BLIND MAN WITH A PISTOL

Also by Chester Himes

Cotton Comes to Harlem
The Crazy Kill
The Heat's On
A Rage in Harlem
The Real Cool Killers

Chester Himes

Blind Man with a Pistol

VINTAGE CRIME / BLACK LIZARD

VINTAGE BOOKS A DIVISION OF RANDOM HOUSE, INC. NEW YORK

First Vintage Books Edition, December 1989

 Published in the United States by Vintage Books, a division of Random House, Inc., New York. Originally published in Great Britain by Allison & Busby Ltd in 1986.

Library of Congress Cataloging-in-Publication Data
Himes, Chester B., 1909–
Blind man with a pistol / Chester Himes.—1st Vintage Books ed.
p. cm.—(Vintage crime)
ISBN: 978-0-394-75998-2
I. Title.
PS3515.I713B58 1989 89-40063
813'.54—dc20 CIP

Manufactured in the United States of America
20 19 18 17 16 15 14

146122990

Preface

A friend of mine, Phil Lomax, told me this story about a blind man with a pistol shooting at a man who had slapped him on a subway train and killing an innocent bystander peacefully reading his newspaper across the aisle and I thought, damn right, sounds just like today's news, riots in the ghettos, war in Vietnam, masochistic doings in the Middle East. And then I thought of some of our loudmouthed leaders urging our vulnerable soul brothers on to getting themselves killed, and thought further that all unorganized violence is like a blind man with a pistol.

CHESTER HIMES

Foreword

"Motherfucking right, it's confusing; it's a gas, baby, you dig."

A Harlem intellectual

I know what you want.
How you know that?
Just lookin at you.
Cause I'm white?
Tain't that. I got the eye.
You think I'm looking for a girl.
Chops is your dish.
Not pork.
Naw.
Not overdone.
Naw. Just right.

"Blink once, you're robbed," Coffin Ed advised the white man slumming in Harlem.
"Blink twice, you're dead," Grave Digger added dryly.

1

On 119th Street there had been a sign for years in the front window of an old dilapidated three-storey brick house, announcing: FUNERALS PERFORMED. For five years past the house had been condemned as unsafe for human habitation. The wooden steps leading up to the cracked, scabby front door were so rotten one had to mount them like crossing a river on a fallen tree trunk; the foundation was crumbling, one side of the house had sunk more than a foot lower than the other, the concrete windowsills had fallen from all the upper windows and the constant falling of bricks from the front wall created a dangerous hazard for passing pedestrians. Most of the windowpanes had long been broken out and replaced with brown wrapping-paper, and the edges of linoleum could be seen hanging from the roof where years before it had been placed there to cover a leak. No one knew what it looked like inside, and no one cared. If any funerals had ever been performed within, it had been before the memory of any residents then on the street.

Police cruisers had passed daily and glanced at it unconcernedly. The cops weren't interested in funerals. Building inspectors had looked the other way. Gas and electric meter readers never stopped, for it had no gas and electricity. But everyone on the street had seen a considerable number of short-haired, black nuns clad in solid black vestments coming and going at all hours of day and night, picking their way up the rotting stairs like cats on a hot tin roof. The colored neighbors just assumed it was a convent, and that it was in such bad repair seemed perfectly reasonable in view of the fact it was obviously a jim-crowded convent, and no one ever dreamed that white Catholics would act any different from anyone else who was white.

It was not until another innocuous card appeared in the window one day, requesting: "Fertile womens, lovin God, inquire within," that anyone had given it a thought. Two white cops in a cruiser who had been driving by the house on their normal patrol every day for the past year were proceeding past as usual when the cop beside the driver shouted, "Whoa, man! You see what I see?"

The driver stamped on the brakes and backed up so he could see too. "Fertile womens . . ." he read. That was as far as he got.

They both had the same thought. What would a colored convent want with "fertile womens"? Fertile womens was for fools, not God.

The inside cop deliberately opened his door, stepped to the sidewalk, adjusted his pistol in its holster and unbuttoned the flap. The driver got out on the street side and came around the car and stood beside his buddy, while performing the same operations with his own pistol. They stared at the sign without expression. They looked at the brown-papered windows. They examined the façade of the whole crumbling edifice as though they had never seen it before.

Then the first cop jerked his head. "Come on."

The second cop followed. When the first cop planted his big foot on the second stair with assured authority, it went on through the rotting wood up to his knee. "Jesus Goddam Christ!" he exclaimed. "These steps are rotten."

The second cop didn't see any need in commenting on the obvious. He hitched up his holster belt and said, "Let's try the back."

As they picked their way around the house through knee-high weeds dense with booby traps of unseen bottles, tin cans, rusted bed springs, broken emery stones, rotting harness, dead cats, dog offal, puddles of stinking garbage, and swarms of bottle flies, house flies, gnats, mosquitoes, the first cop said in extreme disgust, "I don't see how people can live in such filth."

But he hadn't seen anything yet. When they arrived at the back they found a section of the wall had fallen from the second floor, leaving a room exposed to the weather, and the rubble piled on the ground formed the only access to the open back door. Carefully they climbed up the pile of broken bricks and plaster, their footsteps raising a thick gray dust, and entered the kitchen unimpeded.

A fat black man naked to the waist glanced at them casually from muddy eyes which seemed to pop from his wet black face and went on with what he was doing. The old rusted iron floor from a Volkswagen had been placed on four bricks on one side of the warped board floor and a brick firebox had been raised in its center. Sitting on top of a charcoal fire in the firebox was a huge iron pot, blackened by smoke, of a type southern mammies use to boil clothes, filled with some sort of stew which had a strong nauseating smell, being stirred with slow indifference by the sweating black man. The torso of the black man looked like a misshapen lump of crude rubber. He had a round black face with a harelip which caused him to slobber constantly, and his grayish skull was shaved.

Large patches of faded ochre wallpaper, splotched with rust-colored stains and water marks, hung from gray plaster. There were several places where the plaster had fallen off, revealing the brown wooden slats.

"Who's the boss around here, Rastus?" the first cop demanded.

The black man kept stirring his stew as though he hadn't heard.

The cop reddened. He drew his pistol and stepped forward and jabbed the black man in the blubber over his ribs. "Can't you hear?"

Without an obvious change of motion, the ladle rose from the stew and rapped the cop over the head. The second cop leapt foward and hit the black man across his shaved skull with the butt edge of his pistol. The black man grunted and fell onto the old car floor beside the firebox.

A black nun came from another open door and saw the black man lying unconscious beside the stew pot and two white cops standing over him with drawn pistols and screamed. Other black nuns came running, followed by what seemed to be a horde of naked black children. The cops were so shocked their first impulse was to run. But when the first one leapt through the back doorway his foot gave way on the pile of rubble and he slid down into the high weeds of the back yard on the seat of his pants. The second cop turned about in the open doorway and held back the mob with his gun. For a moment he had the odd sensation of having fallen into the middle of the Congo.

The cop outside got up and brushed himself off. "Can you hold 'em while I call the sation?"

"Oh, sure," the second cop said with more confidence than he felt. "They ain't nothing but niggers."

When the first cop returned from radioing the Harlem precinct for reinforcements, a very old man dressed in a spotted long-sleeved white gown had come into the kitchen and cleared out the nuns and the children. He was clean shaven, and his sagging parchment-like skin which seemed but a covering for his skeleton was tight about his face like a leather mask. Wrinkled lids, looking more like dried skin, dropped over his milky bluish eyes, giving him a vague similarity to an old snapping turtle. His cracked voice had a note of mild censure: "He didn't mean no harm, he's a cretin."

"You ought to teach him better than to attack police officers," the cop complained. "Now I smell like I've been ducked in shit."

"He cooks for the children," the old man said. "Sometimes it does smell strange," he admitted.

"It smells like feces," the second cop said. He'd attended City College.

One of the nuns entering the kitchen at just that moment said indignantly, "It is feetsies. Everybody ain't rich like you white folks."

"Now, now, Buttercup, these gentlemen mean no harm," the old man chided. "They but acted in self-defense. They were ignorant of the reactions of Bubber."

"What they doin' here anyway?" she muttered, but a look from him sent her scampering.

"You the boss man, then?" the first cop said.

"Yes, sir, I am Reverend Sam."

"Are you a monk?" the second cop asked.

A smile seemed to twitch the old man's face. "No, I'm a Mormon."

The first cop scratched his head. "What all these nuns doing here then?"

"They're my wives."

"Well, I'll be Goddamned! A nigger Mormon married to a bunch of nigger nuns. And all these children? You running an orphanage too?"

"No, they're my own children. I'm trying to raise them as best the Lord will permit."

The cops looked at him sharply. Both had a strong suspicion he was playing them for fools.

"You mean grandchildren," the cop suggested.

"Great-grandchildren, more like it," the first cop amended.

"No, they're all from the seeds of my loins."

The cops stared at him goggle-eyed. "How old are you, uncle?"

"I believe that I am about a hundred to the best of my knowledge."

They stared at him openmouthed. From the interior of the house they could hear the loud shouting and laughter of children at play and the soft voices of women admonishing them to silence. A feral odor seeped into the kitchen, over and above the smell of the stew. It was a familiar odor and the cop racked his memory to place it. The other cop stared fascinated into the milky bluish eyes of the old man, which reminded him of some milkstones he had seen in a credit jewelry store.

The fat black man was beginning to stir and the cop drew his pistol to be prepared. The fat man rolled over on to his back and looked from the cop to the old man. "Papa, he hit me," he tattled in a voice made barely distinguishable by his slobbery drolling.

"Papa will send away the bad mens, now you go on playing house," the old man croaked. There was a strange note of benevolence when he addressed the cretin.

The cop blinked."Papa!" he echoed. "He your son too?"

Suddenly the second cop snapped his fingers. "The monkey house!" he exclaimed.

"God made us all," Reverend Sam reminded him gently.

"Not them fifty little pickaninnies, according to you," the cop said.

"I am merely God's instrument."

Suddenly the first cop remembered why they had stopped in the first place. "You got a sign in the window, uncle, advertising for fertile women. Ain't you got enough women?"

"I now have only eleven. I must have twelve. One died and she must be replaced."

"Which reminds me, you got another sign in your window saying 'funerals performed'."

The old man looked as near to being surprised as was possible. "Yes, I performed her funeral."

"But that sign's been there for years. I've seen it myself."

"Of course," the old man said. "We all must die."

The cop took off his cap and scratched his blond head. He looked at his partner for advice.

His partner said: "We better wait for the sergeant."

The reinforcements from the Harlem precinct station, headed by a sergeant of detectives, found the remainder of the house in much the same repair as the kitchen. Potbellied coalburning stoves on rusted sheets of metal in the hallways on each floor supplied heat. Light was supplied by homemade lamps without shades made from whiskey bottles. The wives slept on homemade individual pallets, six to a room, on the top floor, while Reverend had his own private room adjoining furnished with a double bed and a chamber pot and little else. There was a large front room on the second floor with all of its windows papered shut where the children slept on loose dirty cotton, evidently the contents of numerous mattresses, which covered the floor from wall to wall about a foot thick.

At the time of their arrival the children were having their lunch, which consisted of the stewed pigsfeet and chitterlings which Bubber, the cretin, had been cooking in the washing pot. It had been divided equally and poured into three rows of troughs in the middle room on the first floor. The naked children were lined up, side by side, on hands and knees, swilling it like pigs.

The detectives counted fifty children, all under the age of ten, and all seemingly healthy. They looked fat enough, with their naked bellies poking out, but several of their burred heads were spotted with tetter, and most of the boys had elongated penises for children so young.

The nuns were gathered about a large bare table in the front room, all busily counting their cheap wooden rosaries, and chanting verses in musical voices which produced a singularly enchanting harmony, but with such indistinct pronunciation that no one could make out the words.

The cretin lay flat on his back on the splintery kitchen floor, his head wrapped in a dirty white bandage stained with mercurochrome, sleeping soundly to the accompaniment of snores that sounded like loud desperate shouts coming from under water. Numerous flies and gnats of all descriptions were feeding on the flow of spittle that drooled from the corners of his harelipped mouth, in preference, seemingly, to the remains of stew in the pot.

In a small room across the hall from where the nuns were sitting, which Reverend Sam called his study, he was being questioned sharply by all twelve cops. Reverend Sam answered their questions politely, looking unperturbed. Yes, he was an ordained minister. Ordained by who? Ordained by God, who else. Yes, the nuns were all his wives. How did he account for that, nuns had made sacred vows to lives of chastity? Yes, there were white nuns and black nuns. What difference did that make? The church provided shelter and food for the white nuns, his black nuns had to hustle for themselves. But religious vows forbid nuns to marry or to participate in any form of carnality. Yes, yes, rightfully speaking, his nuns were virgins. But how could that be when they were his wives and had given birth to, er, fifty children by him? Yes, but being as they were police officers in a sinful world they might not understand; every morning when his wives arose they were virgin nuns, it was only at night, in the dark, that they performed the functions for which God had made their bodies. You mean they were virgins in the morning, nuns during the day, and wives at night? Yes, if you wish to state it in such manner, but you must not overlook the fact that every living person has two beings, the physical and the spiritual, and neither has ascendancy over the other; they could, at best, and with rigid discipline, be carefully separated — which was what he had succeeded doing with his wives. All right, all right, but why didn't his children wear clothes? Why, it was more comfortable without them, and clothes cost money. And eat at tables, like human beings, with knives and forks? Knives and forks cost money, and troughs were more expedient; surely, as white gentlemen and officers of the law, they should understand just what he meant.

The twelve cops reddened to a man. The sergeant, doing most of the questioning, took another tack. What did you want another wife for? Reverend Sam looked up in amazement from beneath his old drooping lids. What a curious question, sir. Shall I answer it? Again the sergeant reddened. Listen, uncle, we're not playing. Neither am I, I assure you, sir. Well, then, what happened to the last one? What last one, sir? The one who died. She died, sir. How, Goddammit? Dead, sir. For what reason? The Lord willed it, sir. Now, listen here, uncle, you're just making it hard on yourself; what was her disease, er, ailment, er, the cause of her death? Childbirth. How old did you say you were? About a hundred, as far as I can determine. All right, you're a hundred; now what did you do with her? We buried her. Where? In the ground. Now listen here, uncle, there are laws about burials; did you have a permit? There are laws for white folks and laws for black folks, sir. All right, all right, but these laws come from God. Which God? There's a white God and there's a black God.

By then, the sergeant had lost his patience. The police continued their investigation without Reverend Sam's assistance. In due course they learned that the household was supported by the wives walking the streets of Harlem, dressed as nuns, begging alms. They also discovered three suspicious-looking mounds in the dirt cellar, which, upon being opened, revealed the remains of three female bodies.

2

It was 2 a.m. in Harlem and it was hot. Even if you couldn't feel it, you could tell it by the movement of the people. Everybody was limbered up, glands lubricated, brains ticking over like a Singer sewing-machine. Everybody was ahead of the play. There wasn't but one square in sight. He was a white man.

He stood well back in the recessed doorway of the United Tobacco store at the northwest corner of 125th Street and Seventh Avenue, watching the sissies frolic about the lunch counter in the Theresa building on the opposite corner. The glass doors had been folded back and the counter was open to the sidewalk.

The white man was excited by the sissies. They were colored and mostly young. They all had straightened hair, conked like silk, waving like the sea; long false eyelashes fringing eyes ringed in mascara; and big cushiony lips painted tan. Their eyes looked naked, brazen, debased, unashamed; they had the greedy look of a sick gourmet. They wore tight-bottomed pastel pants and short-sleeved sport shirts revealing naked brown arms. Some sat to the counter on the high stools, others leaned on their shoulders. Their voices trilled, their bodies moved, their eyes rolled, they twisted their hips suggestively. Their white teeth flashed in brown sweaty faces, their naked eyes steamed in black cups of mascara. They touched one another lightly with their fingertips, compulsively, exclaiming in breathless falsetto, "*Girl. . . .*" Their motions were wanton, indecent, suggestive of an orgy taking place in their minds. The hot Harlem night had brought down their love.

The white man watched them enviously. His body twitched as though he were standing in a hill of ants. His muscles jerked in the strangest places, one side of his face twitched, he had cramps in the right foot, his pants cut his crotch, he bit his tongue, one eye popped out from its socket. One could tell his blood was stirring, but one couldn't tell which way. He couldn't control himself. He stepped out from his hiding place.

At first no one noticed him. He was an ordinary-looking light-haired white man dressed in light gray trousers and a white sport shirt. One could find white men on that corner on any hot night. There was a bright street lamp on each of the four corners of the intersection and cops were always in calling distance. White men were as safe at that intersection as in Times Square. Furthermore they were more welcome.

But the white man couldn't help acting guilty and frightened. He slithered across the street like a moth to the flame. He walked in a one-sided crablike motion, as though submitting only the edge of his body to his inflamed passion. He was watching the frolicsome sissies with such intentness a fast-moving taxi coming east almost ran him down. There was a sudden shriek of brakes, and the loud angry shout of the black driver, "Mother-raper! Ain't you never seen sissies?"

He leapt for the curb, his face burning. All the naked mascaraed eyes about the lunch counter turned on him.

"Ooooo!" a falsetto voice cried delightedly. "A lollipop!"

He drew back to the edge of the sidewalk, face flaming as though he were about to run or cry.

"Don't run, mother," someone said.

White teeth gleamed between thick tan lips. The white man lowered his eyes and followed the edge of the sidewalk around the corner from 125th Street down Seventh Avenue.

"Look, she's blushing," another voice said, setting off a giggle.

The white man looked straight ahead as though ignoring them but when he came to the end of the counter and would have continued past, a heavyset serious man who had been sitting between two empty seats at the end got up to leave, and taking advantage of the distraction the white man slipped into the seat he had vacated.

"Coffee," he ordered in a loud constricted voice. He wanted it to be known that coffee was all he wanted.

The waiter gave him a knowing look. "I know what you want."

The white man forced himself to meet the waiter's naked eyes. "Coffee is all."

The waiter's lips twisted in a derisive grin. The white man noticed they were painted too. He stole a look at the other beauties at the counter. Their huge tan glistening lips looked extraordinarily seductive.

To get his attention the waiter had to speak again. "Chops!" he whispered in a hoarse suggestive voice.

The white man started like a horse shying. "I don't want anything to eat."

"I know."

"Coffee."

"Chops."

"Black."

"Black chops. All you white mothers are just alike."

The white man decided to play ignorant. He acted as though he didn't know what the waiter was talking about. "Are you discriminating against me?"

"Lord, no. Black chops — coffee, I mean — coming right up."

A sissie moved into the seat beside the white man, and put his hand on his leg. "Come with me, mother."

The white man pushed the hand away and looked at him haughtily. "Do I know you?"

The sissie sneered. "Hard to get, eh?"

The waiter looked around from the coffee urn. "Don't bother my customers," he said.

The sissie reacted as though they had a secret understanding. "Oh, like that?"

"Jesus Christ, what's going on?" the white man blurted.

The waiter served him his black coffee. "As if you didn't know," he whispered.

"What's this fad?"

"Ain't they beautiful?"

"What?"

"All them hot tan chops."

The white man's face flamed again. He lifted his cup of coffee. His hand shook so it slopped over on the counter.

"Don't be nervous," the waiter said. "You got it made. Put down your money and take your choice."

Another man slipped on to the end stool next to the white man. He was a thin black man with a long smooth face. He wore black pants, a black long-sleeved shirt with black buttons and a bright red fez. There was a wide black band around the fez with the large white-lettered words, BLACK POWER. He might have been a Black Muslim but for the fact Black Muslims avoided the vicinity of perverts and were hardly ever seen at that lunch counter. And the bookstore diagonally across Seventh Avenue where Black Muslims sometimes assembled and held mass meetings had been closed since early the previous evening, and the Black Muslim temple was nine blocks south on 116th Street. But he was dressed like one and he was black enough. He leaned toward the white man and whispered in his other ear, "I know what you want."

The waiter gave him a look. "Chops," he said.

As he leaned away from the black man, the white man thought they were all talking in a secret language. All he wanted was to get with the sissies, the tan-lipped brownbodied girl-boys, strip off his clothes, let himself be ravished. The thought made him weak as water, dissolved his bones, dizzied his head. He refused to think more than that. And the waiter and this other ugly black man were destroying that, cooling his ardor, wetting him down. He became angry. "Let me alone, I know what I want," he said.

"Bran," the black man said.

"Chops," the waiter said.

"It's breakfast time," the black man said. "The man wants breakfast food. Without bones."

Angrily the white man reached back and drew his wallet from his hip pocket. He pulled out a ten-dollar bill from a thick sheaf of notes and threw it on to the counter.

Everyone all up and around the counter stared from the bill to the white man's red angry face.

The waiter had become absolutely still. He let the bill lie. "Ain't you got nothing smaller than that, boss?"

The white man fished in his side pockets. The waiter and the black man in the red fez exchanged glances from the corners of

their eyes. The white man brought out his hands empty.
"I haven't any change," he said.
The waiter picked up the ten-dollar bill and snapped it, held it up to the light and scrutinized it. Satisfied, he put it in the till and made change. He slapped the change down on to the counter in front of the white man, leaning foward. He whispered, "You can go with him, he's safe."
The white man glanced briefly at the black man beside him. The black man grinned obsequiously. The white man picked up his change. It was five dollars short. Holding it in his hand, he looked up into the waiter's eyes. The waiter returned his look, challengingly, shrugged and licked his lips. The white man smiled to himself, all his confidence restored.
"Chops," he admitted.
The black man got up with the vague suggestive movements of an old darky retainer, and began to walk slowly south on Seventh Avenue, past the entrance to the Theresa building. The white man followed but in a short pace he had drawn even with the black man and they went down the street conversing, a black-clad black man in a red fez announcing BLACK POWER and a light-haired white man in gray pants and white shirt, the steerer and the John.

Interlude

Where 125th Street crosses Seventh Avenue is the Mecca of Harlem. To get established there, an ordinary Harlem citizen has reached the promised land, if it merely means standing on the sidewalk.

One Hundred and Twenty-fifth Street connects the Triborough Bridge on the east with the former Hudson River Ferry into New Jersey on the west. Crosstown buses ply up and down the street at the rate of one every ten minutes. White motorists passing over the complex toll bridge from the Bronx, Queens or Brooklyn sometimes have occasion to pass through Harlem to the ferry,

Broadway or other destinations, instead of turning downtown via the East Side Drive.

Seventh Avenue runs from the north end of Central Park to the 155th Street Bridge where the motorists going north to Westchester County and beyond cross over the Harlem River into the Bronx and the Grand Concorse. The Seventh Avenue branch of the Fifth Avenue bus line passes up and down this section of Seventh Avenue and turns over to Fifth Avenue on 100th Street at the top of Central Park and goes south down Fifth Avenue to Washington Square.

Therefore many white people riding the buses or in motor cars pass this corner daily. Furthermore, most of the commercial enterprises — stores, bars, restaurants, theaters, etc. — and real estate are owned by white people.

But it is the Mecca of the black people just the same. The air and the heat and the voices and the laughter, the atmosphere and the drama and the melodrama, are theirs. Theirs are the hopes, the schemes, the prayers and the protest. They are the managers, the clerks, the cleaners, they drive the taxis and the buses, they are the clients, the customers, the audience; they work it, but the white man owns it. So it is natural that the white man is concerned with their behavior; it's his property. But it is the black people's to enjoy. The black people have the past and the present, and they hope to have the future.

The old Theresa Hotel, where once the greatest of the black had their day in the luxury suites overlooking the wide, park-divided sweep of Seventh Avenue, or in the large formal dining-room where dressing for dinner was mandatory, or in the dark cozy intimacy of the bar where one could see the greatest of the singers, jazz musicians, politicians, educators, prize fighters, racketeers, pimps, prostitutes. Memory calls up such names as Josephine Baker, Florence Mills, Lady Day, Bojangles Bill Robinson, Bert Williams, Chick Webb, Lester Young, Joe Louis, Henry Armstrong, Congressmen Dawson and De-Priest, educators Booker T. Washington and Charles Johnson, writers Bud Fisher, Claude MacKay, Countee Cullen, and others too numerous to mention. And their white friends and sponsors: Carl Van

Vechten, Rebecca West, Dodd, Dodge, Rockefeller. Not to mention the movie actors and actresses of all races, the unforgettable Canada Lee and John Garfield.

3

Motorists coming west on 125th Street from the Triborough Bridge saw a speaker standing in the tonneau of an old muddy battered US Army command car, parked in the amber night light at the corner of Second Avenue, in front of a sign which read: *CHICKEN AUTO INSURANCE, Seymour Rosenblum.* None had the time or interest to investigate further. The white motorists thought that the Negro speaker was selling "chicken auto insurance" for Seymour Rosenblum. They could well believe it. "*Chicken*" had to do with the expression, "Don't be chicken!" and that was the way people drove in Harlem.

But actually the "chicken" sign was left over from a restaurant that had gone bankrupt and closed months previously, and the sign advertising auto insurance had been placed across the front of the closed shop afterwards.

Nor was the speaker selling auto insurance, which was farther from his thoughts than chicken. He had merely chosen that particular spot because he had felt he was least likely to be disturbed by the police. The speaker was named Marcus Mackenzie, and he was a serious man. Although young, slender and handsome, Marcus Mackenzie was as serious as an African Methodist minister with one foot in the grave. Marcus Mackenzie's aim was to save the world. But before then, it was to solve the Negro Problem. Marcus Mackenzie believed brotherhood would do both. He had assembled a group of young white and black people to march across the heart of Harlem on 125th Street from Second Avenue on the east to Convent Avenue on the west. He had been preparing this march for more than six months. He had begun the previous December when he had returned from

Europe after spending two years in the US Army in Germany. He had learned all the necessary techniques in the army. Hence the old command car. One commanded best from a command car. That was what they were designed for. Kept you high off the ground, better to deploy your forces. Also it would carry all the first-aid equipment that might be needed: plasma, surgical instruments, cat gut for sutures, snakebite medicine which he felt would be just as effective for rat bites — which were more likely in Harlem — rubber raincoats in case of rain, black greasepaint for his white marchers to quickly don blackfaces in an emergency.

Most of the young men waiting to take formations of squads wore tee shirts and shorts. For now it was July 15th. Getaway day. Nat Turner day. There were only forty-eight of them. But Marcus Mackenzie believed that from little acorns big oaks grew. Now he was giving his marchers a last pep talk before the march began. He was speaking over a portable amplifier as he stood in the tonneau of the command car. But many other people had stopped to listen, for his voice carried far and wide. People who lived in the neighborhood. Black people, and white people too, for that far east on 125th Street was still a racially mixed neighborhood. The elderly people, for the most part, were the heads of families; the younger people in their twenties might be anything, black and white alike. There were many prostitutes, pederasts, pickpockets, sneak thieves, confidence men, steerers, and pimps in the area who served the 125th Street railroad station two blocks away. But Marcus Mackenzie had no tolerance for these.

"*The greatest boon to mankind that history will ever know can be brotherly love,*" he was saying. "*Brotherhood! It can be more nutritious than bread. More warming than wine. More soothing than song. More satisfying than sex. More beneficial than science. More curing than medicine.*" The metaphors might have been mixed and the delivery stilted, for Marcus was not highly educated. But no one could doubt the sincerity in his voice. The sincerity was so pure it was heart-breaking. Everyone within earshot was touched by his sincerity. "*Man's love for man. Let me tell you, it is like all religions put together, like all the gods embracing. It is the greatest. . . .*"

No one doubted him. The intensity of his emotion left no room for doubt. But one elderly black man, equally serious, standing on the opposite side of the street, expressed his concern and that of others. "I believe you, son. But how you gonna get it to work?"

"We're going to march!" Marcus declared in a ringing voice.

Whether that answered the old man's question or not was never known. But it answered Marcus Mackenzie's. He had given a lot of thought to the question. It seemed as though his whole life had been lived only to supply this answer. His earliest memory was of the Detroit race riot in 1943, right during the middle of the United States fierce fight against other forms of racism in other countries. But he had been too young to comprehend this irony. All he remembered was his father going in and out of their apartment in the ghetto, the shouting and gunshots from the unseen street, and his elder sister sitting in the front room of their closed and shuttered flat with a big black revolver in her lap pointed at the door. He had been four years old and she seven. They had been alone all the times their father had been out trying to rescue other black people from the police. Their mother was dead. When he had become old enough to know the diffrence between the "North" and the "South" he had become terrified. Mainly because Detroit was about as far north as one could go. And it had seemed as though he had suffered all the same restrictions there, the same abuses, the same injustices, as his black brothers in the South. He had lived all his life in a black slum, had attended jim-crowed schools, and after graduating from high school had got the customary jim-crow job in a factory. Then he had been drafted into the army and sent to Germany. It was there he had learned the techniques of the march, although for the most part he had served as an orderly in the women's maternity ward of the US Army hospital in Wiesbaden. He had been very much alone as there were no other Negroes working in the hospital at the same hours. He read only the Bible and he had lots of time to think. He was treated well by the white staff and expectant mothers who, in his ward, were wives of officers, most of whom were from the South. He knew there was little social integration in the army and what there was among GIs was rigidly enforced. The Negro

Problem existed there as it had everywhere else he had ever lived. But still he was treated well. He came to the conclusion that it was all a matter of black and white people getting to know each other. He was not a very bright boy and he never knew he had been selected for the job because of his neat, clean-cut appearance. He was tall and slender with sepia skin and a long softly angled face. His eyes were brown. His black hair, worn very short, was straight at the roots. He had always been very serious. He was never frivolous. He seldom smiled. By the time he had served two years, mostly in the company of white people who treated him well, a great deal alone, reading and studying the Old and New Testaments of the Bible, he had come to the conclusion that plain Christian love was the solution to the Negro Problem. But he had learned plenty about marching. For a time he entertained the grandiose idea of returning to the States and imbuing all the inhabitants with Christian love. But he soon discovered that Doctor Martin Luther King had beat him to the idea and he sought about in his mind for something else.

After his discharge he went to Paris to live until his money ran out, as did a great number of other discharged GIs. He got a room with another young brother in a hotel on Rue Chaplain, around the corner from Boulevard Raspail and Montparnasse, almost within hailing distance of the *Rotonde* and the *Dôme*. It was a hotel very popular with discharged Negro GIs in Paris, partly because of its location and partly because of the army of prostitutes who cruised from there under a strict discipline similar to that they'd just left. He knew no one but other discharged GIs, all of whom recognized one another on sight, whether they had met before or not. They comprised an unofficial club; they talked the same language, ate the same food, went to the same places — usually to the cheap restaurants by day and the movie theater — *Studio Parnasse* — down the street, or Buttercup's Chicken Shack over on Rue Odessa at night. They gathered in each others' rooms and discussed the situation back home. Mostly they talked of the various brothers back home who had struck it rich and made the bigtime via the Negro Problem. Most of them had no trade or profession or education in any specific field, if indeed any at all. As a consequence, whether they admitted it or not, most of them were resolved to get a foothold in this bonanza. They felt if they could just somehow get involved in the Negro Problem, the next step up the ladder would be good paying jobs in government or private industry. All they needed was an idea. "Look at Martin Luther King. What's he done?" . . . "He done got rich. That's what." But Marcus had no patience for cynicism. He felt it was sacrilege. He was pure in heart. He wanted the Negroes to arise. He wanted to lead them out of the abyss into the promised land. The trouble was, he wasn't very bright.

Then one night at Buttercup's he met this Swedish woman, Birgit, who was famous for her glass. She had dropped in to look over the brothers. She and Marcus found their affinity immediately. Both of them were serious, both were seeking, both were extraordinarily stupid. But she taught him brotherly love. She was hipped on brotherly love. Although it didn't mean the same thing to her as it did to him. She had had a number of brothers as lovers and in time she had become enthusiastic about brotherly love. But Marcus had the vision of Brotherhood.

The same night he met her, he gave up on the idea of plain Christian love. Buttercup was sitting at a big table where she could oversee the entrance, the bar and the dance floor at the same time, surrounded as usual by a number of sycophants, like a big fat mother hen with a brood of wet chicks and ugly ducklings, and she had introduced Marcus to Birgit, seeing as they were both serious, both seeking. At one end of the same table a fattish erudite white man vacationing from his teaching post in Black Africa was holding forth on the economy of the new African states. Feeling the man was getting too much of Birgit's attention, as he had just met her and didn't as yet know about her brotherly love, Marcus sought to steer the conversation away from Black African economy to the American Negro Problem where he could shine. He wanted to shine for Birgit. He didn't know he already shone to her satisfaction. Suddenly he interrupted the man. He held forth his Bible, dangling the gold cross. He was absorbed by Christian love. "What does that mean to you?" he challenged, pointing to the cross, preparing to expound his brilliant idea. The man looked from the cross to Marcus's face. He smiled sadly. He said, "It don't mean a damn thing to me, I'm a Jew." Right then and there Marcus dropped his ideas on Christian love. He was ready for brotherly love when Birgit took him home. But he was serious.

Birgit took him to live with her in the South of France. She had a good business in glassware and was famous. But she was more interested in the welfare of the American Negro than in glass. She was a perfect foil to the wild ideas of Marcus. They spent most of their waking hours discussing ways and means to solve this problem. Once she declared she would become the richest and most famous woman in the world and then she would go to the American South and call a press conference and let it be known that she lived with a Negro. But Marcus didn't think much of that idea. He felt she should be in the background and he should take the lead. It was inevitable that two such wildly enthusiastic people would have some misunderstandings. But the only serious one they had was about the correct way to stand on one's head. She did it her way. He said it was wrong. They argued. He was stubborn. She pointed out that she was older than he was, and heavier. He left her and went back to Detroit. She hopped on a plane and went to Detroit and took him back to France. It was after then that he became convinced of the efficacy of Brotherly Love. He woke up one morning with a vision of Brotherhood. In this vision he saw it solving all the problems of the world. He already knew about the March. That much the US Army had taught him. Put the two together and they'd work, he concluded.

The next week he and Birgit arrived in New York and took a room in the Texas Hotel near the 125th Street station and went into the business of organizing the "March of Brotherhood".

Now the moment had arrived. Birgit took her place beside him in the command car. She pulled up her large striped cotton dirndl skirt made by her fellow national, Katya of Sweden, and looked around with an excited smile. But to onlookers it was more like the strained expression of a Swedish farm woman in a Swedish outhouse in the dead of a Swedish winter. She was trying to restrain her excitement at the sight of all those naked limbs in the amber light. From the shoulders up she had the delicate neckline and face of a Nordic goddess, but below her body was breastless, lumpy with bulging hips and huge round legs like sawed-off telegraph posts. She felt elated, sitting there with her man who was leading these colored people in this march for their rights. She loved colored people. Her eyeblue eyes gleamed with this love. When she looked at the white cops her lips curled with scorn.

A number of police cruisers had appeared at the moment the march was to begin. They stared at the white woman and the colored man in the command car. Their lips compressed but they said nothing, did nothing. Marcus had got a police permit.

The marchers lined up four abreast on the right side of the street, facing west. The command car was at the lead. Two police cars brought up the rear. Three were parked at intervals down the street as far as the railroad station. Several others cruised slowly in the westbound traffic, turned north at Lenox Avenue, east again on 126th Street, back to 125th Street on Second Avenue and retraced the route. The chief inspector had said he didn't want any trouble in Harlem.

"Squads, MARCH!" Marcus shouted over the amplifier.

The black youth driving the old Dodge car slipped in the clutch. The white youth sitting at his side raised his arms with his hands clasped in the sign of brotherhood. The old command car shuddered and moved off. The forty-eight integrated black and white marchers stepped forward, their black and white legs flashing in the amber lights of the bridge approach. Their bare black and white arms shone. Their silky and kinky heads glistened. Marcus had been careful to select black youths who were black and white youths who were white. Somehow the black against the white and the white against the black gave the illusion of nakedness. The forty-eight orderly young marchers gave the illusion of an orgy. The black and white naked flesh in the amber light filled the black and white onlookers with a strange excitement. Cars slowed down and white people leaned out the windows. Black people walking down the street grinned, then laughed, then shouted encouragement. It was as though an unseen band had struck up a Dixieland march. The colored people on the sidewalks on both sides of the street began locomotioning and boogalooing as though gone mad. White women in the passing automobiles screamed and waved frantically. Their male companions turned red like a race of boiled lobsters. The police cars opened their sirens to clear the traffic. But it served to call the attention of more people from the sidelines.

When the marchers came abreast of the 125th Street station on upper Park Avenue, a long straggling tail of laughing, dancing, hysterical black and white people had attached itself to the original forty-eight. Black and white people came from the station waiting-room to stare in popeyed amazement. Black and white people came from nearby bars, from the dim stinking doorways, from the flea-bag hotels, from the cafeterias, the greasy spoons, from the shoe-shine parlors, the poolrooms – pansies and prostitutes, ordinary bar drinkers and strangers in the area who had stopped for a bit to eat, Johns and squares looking for excitement, muggers and sneak thieves looking for victims. The scene that greeted them was like a carnival. It was a hot night. Some of them were drunk. Others had nothing to do. They joined the carnival group thinking maybe they were headed for a revival meeting, a sex orgy, a pansy ball, a beer festival, a baseball game. The white people attracted by the black. The black people attracted by the white.

Marcus looked back from his command car and saw a whole sea of white and black humanity in his wake. He was exultant. He had made it. He knew all people needed was a chance to love one another.

He clutched Birgit's thigh and shouted, "I've made it, baby. Just look at 'em! Tomorrow my name will be in all the papers."

She looked back at the wild following, then she gave him a melting look of love. "My man! You're so intelligent. It's just like Walpurgisnacht."

4

The Negro detectives, Grave Digger Jones and Coffin Ed Johnson, were making their last round through Harlem in the old black Plymouth sedan with the unofficial tag, which they used as their official car. In the daytime it might have been recognized, but at night it was barely distinguishable from any number of other dented, dilapidated struggle buggies cherished by the citizens of Harlem; other than when they had to go somewhere in a hurry it went. But now they were idling along, west on 123rd Street, with the lights out as was their custom on dark side streets. The car scarcely made a sound; for all its dilapidated appearance the motor was ticking almost silently. It passed along practically unseen, like a ghostly vehicle floating in the dark, its occupants invisible.

This was due in part to the fact that both detectives were almost as dark as the night, and they were wearing lightweight black alpaca suits and black cotton shirts with the collars open. Whereas other people were in shirt sleeves on this hot night, they wore their suit coats to cover the big glinting nickel-plated thirty-eight-caliber revolvers they wore in their shoulder slings. They could see in the dark streets like cats, but couldn't be seen, which was just as well because their presence might have discouraged the vice business in Harlem and put countless citizens on relief.

Actually they weren't concerned with prostitution or its feeder vices, unlicensed clubs, bottle peddlers, petty larceny, short con and steering. They had no use for pansies, but as long as they didn't hurt anyone, pansies could pansy all they pleased. They weren't arbiters of sex habits. There was no accounting for the sexual tastes of people. Just don't let anyone get hurt.

If white citizens wished to come to Harlem for their kicks, they had to take the venereal risks and the risks of short con or having their money stolen. Their only duty was to protect them from violence.

They went down the side street without lights to surprise anyone in the act of maiming, mugging, rolling drunks, or committing homicide.

They knew the first people to turn on them if they tried to keep the white man out of Harlem after dark would be the whores themselves, the madams, the pimps, the proprietors of the late-hour joints, most of whom were paying off some of their colleagues on the force.

For such a hot night, Harlem had been exceptionally peaceful. No riots, no murders, only a few cars stolen, which wasn't their business, and a few domestic cuttings.

They were taking it easy.

"It's been a quiet night," Coffin Ed said from his seat by the sidewalk.

"Better touch wood," Grave Digger replied, lazily steering with one hand.

"There ain't any wood in this tin lizzie."

"There's the baseball bat that man was beating his old lady with."

"Hell, bats are made of plastic these days. Too bad we ain't got his head."

"Lots of them around. Next one we come to I'll stop."

"How about that one?"

Grave Digger looked ahead through the windscreen and saw the back of a black man in a black ensemble with a red fez stuck on his head. He knew the man hadn't seen them as yet nevertheless he was running as though he meant it. The man was carrying a pair of light gray pants over one arm with the legs blowing in the breeze as though they were running too, but a little faster.

"Look at that boy picking 'em up and laying 'em down like the earth was red-hot."

"Reckon we ought to ask him?" Coffin Ed said.

"What for? To hear him lie? The white man who owned those pants ought to have kept them on."

Coffin Ed chuckled. "You said the next one we came to you'd stop."

"Yeah, and you said it was quiet too. Let's keep it that way. What's unusual about a black brother stealing a whitey's pants who's laying up somewhere with a black whore?"

They were relaxed and indifferent. It wasn't their business to rescue the pants of a white man who was stupid enough to let them be stolen. They knew of too many cases where the white John went in the room and left his trousers draped over a chair by the door — with his money in it.

"The first thing to learn about whore-chasing is what to do with your money while screwing."

"That's simple," Grave Digger said. "Leave what you don't need at home."

"And let your old lady find it? What's the difference?"

They let the fez-headed man get out of sight while they shot the bull. Suddenly Coffin Ed blurted, "It ain't quiet no more."

A bareheaded white man had materialized suddenly from the darkness into the dim pool of yellow light spilling from a street lamp, trying to run in the direction taken by the black man. But he staggered on wobbly legs as though drunk. They could see his legs plainly because he didn't wear any pants. In fact he didn't wear any underpants either and they could see his bare white ass beneath his white shirttail.

Grave Digger switched on the headlamps and the next instant he stepped on the accelerator. The car pulled to the curb beside the staggering man with the scream of tires on pavement, and both big double-jointed detectives emerged from opposite sides of the car like hoboes alighting from a moving freight. For an instant there was only the sound of flat feet slapping on concrete as they converged upon the tottering white man from fore and aft. Coming up from the front side Grave Digger drew his torch. It was a rapid dangerous-looking motion until the light hit the white man's face. Grave Digger drew up sharp. Coffin Ed, coming from the rear, pinioned the white man's arms.

"Hold him steady," Grave Digger said, fishing out his shield and turning the light on it. "We're policemen. You're safe."

Even while saying it he thought it was a stupid thing to say. The front of the white man's shirt was covered with blood. More blood spurted from the side of his throat where his jugular had been cut.

The white man shuddered convulsively and began sinking to the ground. Coffin Ed held him up. "What's the matter with him?" he asked. He couldn't see from behind.

"Throat cut."

The white man's mouth was clamped shut as though he were holding in his life. Blood spurted from the wound at every third or fourth heartbeat. Drops trickled from his nose. His eyes were beginning to glaze.

"Lay him on his back," Grave Digger said.

Coffin Ed lowered the body full-length on its back down the dirty pavement. Both of them could see that life was going fast. He was not a pretty sight stretched out in the headlight glare. There was no chance of saving his life. That urgency had passed. Now there was a different urgency. It sounded in Grave Digger's voice as he bent over the dying man, thick, constricted, cottony dry:

"Quick! Quick! Who did it?"

The glazing eyes of the dying man gave no sign of comprehension, only the grim, clamped mouth tightened slightly.

Grave Digger bent closer to hear should the clamped lips open. Blood spurted from the man's cut throat into his face, suddenly nauseating him with its sweet, sickish scent. But he ignored it as he tried to hold the man on to life by his eyes.

"Quick!" Urgent, dry, compelling. "A name? Give us a name!" His jaw muscles rippled over gritted teeth.

A last brief flicker of comprehension showed in the white man's eyes. For an infinitesimal instant the pupils contracted slightly. The man was making a tremendous effort to speak. The strain was visible in a slight tightening of the muscles of the face and neck.

"Who did it? Quick! A name!" Grave Digger hammered, his black face bloody and contorted.

The white man's tightly clamped lips trembled and suddenly opened, like a seldom used door. A liquid, gurgling sound came out, followed instantly by a gush of blood in which he drowned.

" '*Jesus,*' " Grave Digger echoed as he slowly straightened his bent figure. " '*Jesus bastard!*' What a thing to say."

Coffin Ed's face was like a thundercloud. "Jesus, Digger, Goddammit!" he flared. "What you want him to say, Jesus hallelujah? The mother-raper got his throat cut for a black whore—"

"How you know it was a black whore who did it?"

"By whoever!"

"All right, let's call the precinct," Grave Digger said thoughtfully, playing his flashlight over the dead man's body. "Male, fair hair — blue eyes; jugular vein cut, dead on 123rd Street —" Glancing at his watch. "3.11 a.m.," he recited.

Coffin Ed had hurried back to the car to get the precinct station on the radio. "Without his pants," he added.

"Later."

While Coffin Ed was transmitting the essential facts over the radio-phone, colored people in various stages of undress began emerging from the black dark tenements alongside. Black women in terrycloth robes with their faces greased and their straightened hair done in small tight plaits like Topsy; brownskinned women with voluptuous breasts and broad buttocks wrapped in bright-coloured nylon, half-straight hair hanging loosely about their cushion-mouthed sleepy-eyed faces; high yellows in their silks and curlers. And the men, old, young, nappy-headed, conk-haired, eyes full of sleep, faces lined where witches were riding them, mouths slack, wrapped in sheets, blankets, raincoats, or just soiled and wrinkled pajamas. Collecting in the street to see the dead man. Looking inexpressibly stupid in their morbid curiosity. A dead man was always good to see. It was reassuring to see somebody else dead. Generally the dead men were also colored. A white dead man was really something. Worth getting up any time of night. But no one asked who cut him. Nor why. Who was going to ask who cut a white man's throat in Harlem? Or why? Just look at him, baby. And feel good it ain't you. Look at that white mother-raper with his throat cut. You know what he was after. . . .

Coffin Ed gave Lieutenant Anderson a brief description of the dead body and a more detailed description of the black man in the red fez they had first seen running down the street with the pants over his arm.

"Do you think the murdered man had some extra pants?" Anderson asked.

"He didn't have *any* pants."

"What the hell!" Anderson exclaimed. "What the hell's wrong with you? What are you holding back? Let's have it all."

"The man didn't have any pants or underpants."

"Mmmm. All right, Johnson, you and Jones stay put. I'll call homicide, the District Attorney and the Medical Examiner and have them send their men, and I'll put out a pickup for the suspect. You think I should seal up the block?"

"What for? If the suspect did it, he'll be to hell and gone by the time you get the block sealed off. And if anybody else did it they were already gone. All you can do is take in a couple loads of these citizens for questioning if we can determine exactly where it was done."

"All right, in time. Right now you and Jones stay with the body and see what you can learn."

"What'd the boss say?" Grave Digger asked when Coffin Ed rejoined him beside the body on the sidewalk.

"Just the usual. The experts are coming. We're to dig what we can without leaving our friend."

Grave Digger turned towards the silent crowd collecting in the shadows. "Any of you know anything that might help?"

"H. Exodus Clay is the name of an undertaker," a brother said.

"Does this look like a time for that?"

"To me it does. When a man's dead you got to bury him."

"I mean anything that might help find out who killed him," Grave Digger said to the others.

"I seen a white man and a colored man whispering."

"Where was that, lady?"

"Eighth Avenue at 15th Street."

People in Harlem always drop the "one hundred" from the designation of their streets, so that 10th Street is 110th, 15th is 115th and 25th is 125th. That wasn't very near but it was close enough.

"When, lady?"

"I don't remembers 'zactly. Night 'fore last, I thinks."

"All right, forget it. You folks go to bed."

A little shuffling followed but no one left.

"Shit!" someone exclaimed.

"Those car cops must be sleeping," Coffin Ed said impatiently.

Grave Digger began a cursory examination of the body. There was a cut across the back of the left hand and a deep cut in the palm of the right hand between the index finger and thumb. "He tried to ward off the knife first, then he grabbed the blade. He wasn't very scared."

"How you make that?"

"Hell, if he'd been trying to run, ducking and dodging, he'd been cut on the arms and back if his throat hadn't been cut to start with, as you can see it hadn't."

"All right, Sherlock Jones. Then tell me this much. How come his privates ain't been touched? If this was a sex fight that's the first thing they go for."

"How we know it was a sex fight? It was probably plain robbery."

"Well, buddy-o, you can't overlook the fact the man ain't got no pants."

"Yeah, there's that, and this is Harlem, if you want to add it up that way," Grave Digger said. "I just wish these mother-rapers wouldn't come up here and get themselves killed, for whatever reason."

"Iss bad enough killing our own," a voice said from the dark. It was followed by a sudden indistinct babble as though the spectators were arguing the point.

Coffin Ed turned on them and shouted suddenly, "You people better get the hell away from here before the white cops come in, or they'll run all your asses in."

There was a sound of nervous movement, like frightened cattle in the dark, then a voice said belligerently, "Run whose ass in? I lives here!"

"All right," Coffin Ed said resignedly. "Don't say I didn't warn you."

Grave Digger was staring at the stretch of sidewalk where the body lay in a widening pool of blood. The headlights of their car starkly lighted the stretch down past the street lamp and the front steps of a number of crumbling houses on that side of the street that had been private residences of a sort a half-century previous. The people who had collected stood along the other side of the street and in back of their car so their dark faces were in the shadow but a row of rusty bare legs and splayed black feet with enormous toes were visible. A Harlem sidewalk, he thought, black feet and purple blood, and a man lying dead. This time he happened to be white. Most times he was black like the legs and feet of the people who stared at him. How many people had he seen lying dead in the street? He couldn't remember, only that most of them had been black. Lying dead and without dignity on the dirty sidewalks. Lying in the coins of dried spit, sticky ice cream and candy wrappers, wads of chewed gum, stained cigarette butts, newspaper scraps, small bones from cooked meat, dog shit, urine stinks, beer bottles, hair-grease tins; stinking, gritty dirt blowing over them by every puff of wind.

"Anyway, no used condoms," Coffin Ed said. "They don't like it if there ain't no risk."

"Damn right," Grave Digger agreed. "All you got to do is look around and see how many times they've lost."

The first of the sirens sounded.

"Here they are," Coffin Ed said.

The spectators moved back.

Interlude

"Like him?" Doctor Mubuta asked.

"He's beautiful," the white woman said.

"Wrap him up and take him with you," Doctor Mubuta said, coming as near to leering as he had ever done.

She blushed furiously.

Doctor Mubuta motioned to the cretin, who had no

compunction about wrapping up the sleeping beauty in the bed sheet.

"Take him out and put him into the back of her car," Doctor Mubuta directed. Then, turning to the blushing, speechless Mrs Dawson, he said, "He is now your responsibility, Madame. And I trust that as soon as you have thoroughly investigated this miracle and convinced yourself of its authenticity, you will remit the balance of payment."

She nodded quickly and left. They all watched her leave. No one said anything. No one on the street gave a second look at the black harelipped cretin placing a sheet-wrapped figure into the back compartment of an air-conditioned Cadillac limousine. It was Harlem, where anything might happen.

5

"You've been trying to outsmart the white folks, and you found that didn't do no good cause they're smarter than you are," Doctor Mubuta was saying in his singsong voice, his heavy jaw moving with the lecherous twist of a big black whore shaking her butt. His voice was as solemn as his expression and his eyes were as humorless as those of a religious fanatic.

"Yeh!" The obscene twist of his jaw was caught, like one buttock aslant, then it resumed its suggestive grind: "And you've been trying to out-lie the white folk, only to discover it was the white folks who invented lying."

The teen-aged white girl broke out of her hypnotic trance and giggled like she'd been caught out.

Everyone else was staring at him with open mouths as though he were exposing himself.

"Yeh! And you've been trying to out-Tom the white folks, and you're surprised to find the white folks is stealing your talent, like they has stole everything you has invented."

Mister Sam's old rheumy eyes opened at that and he peeped at Doctor Mubuta. But he shut them immediately as though he didn't want to see what he saw. Dick's head moved slightly and an expression of pained cynicism flickered across his face. A subtle smile tugged at the corners of Anny's mouth. Intolerable outrage took hold of Viola's expression. Sugartit's stretched black eyes remained unchanged as though she weren't tuned in. Van Raff seemed to be smoldering at the incredible theft. The teen-aged white girl giggled again and tried to catch Doctor Mubuta's eye. Suddenly he looked directly at her; his vision lost its vague sightless scope and focused on her, his bright red eyes stripping off her clothes and looking directly between her thighs.

"Yeh!" He might have said, "Yeh, man!"

The ejaculation made her start guiltily. She closed her legs and blushed.

Mister Sam seemed to be sleeping, or else dead.

Then they were all listening again, like passengers in a runaway bus, not knowing where they were going but expecting momentarily to run off the edge of the earth.

Doctor Mubuta's expression went vacant again as though he had made his point, whatever it was.

"Yeh! You've been trying to out-yes white folks, but the white folks is yessing you so fast nowadays you don't know who's yessing who."

"Shit!" Until then the speaker had been so inconspicuous he had passed for a gray shadow in the brightly lighted room.

The word was heard distinctly but not one hypnotized gaze switched from Doctor Mubuta's belly-dancing under-jaw.

"Hear those shots?" asked Doctor Mubuta, ignoring the ejaculation.

The question was theoretical. They had been hearing the sound of sporadic shooting for some time and they all knew black youths were rioting on Seventh Avenue. It required no answer.

"Throwing rocks at the police," Doctor Mubuta said in his same singsong voice. "Must think those white police is made of window glass."

He paused for a moment as though inviting comment. But no

one had anything to say; no one knew where it was leading to; they all knew white police were not made of window glass.

"I have the one and only solution for the Negro Problem," Doctor Mubuta exclaimed, his heavy black belly-bumping jaw suddenly throwing it to the wind.

That was the one for someone to challenge him, but no one did.

"We're gonna outlive the white folks. While they has been concentrating on ways of death, I has been concentrating on how to extend life. While they'll be dying, we'll be living forever, and Mister Sam here, the oldest of us all, will be alive to see the day when the black man is the majority on this earth, and the white man his slave."

The teen-aged white girl stared at Doctor Mubuta as though she took it personally, and was even anxious to give it a try.

But not so with Mister Sam's chauffeur, Johnson X, the invisible man. He could hold it no longer. "Shit!" he cried. "Shit!" One couldn't tell whether it was an order or an exclamation. "Shit! Does anyone in their right state of mind, with all their pieces of gray matter assembled in the right way in they haid, with no fuses blowed in they brain, with they think-piece hitting on all cylinders — you dig me? Anyone — you — me — us — they — we — them — him or her — anyone — you dig me? believe that shittt?" His loose lips punctuated each word with a spray of spit, flapped up and down over white buck teeth like the shutter of a camera photographing missiles shot into space, curled and popped over the tonal effect of each sound, and pronounced the word "shit" as though he had tasted it and spat it out — eloquent, logical and positive.

"I believe it," Mister Sam croaked, peeking at Johnson from his old furtive eyes.

"You!" Johnson exploded. It was an accusation.

Everyone stared at Mister Sam as though awaiting his confession.

"Niggers'll believe anything," Viola spluttered. No one contradicted.

Johnson X looked scornfully at Mister Sam from thick-lensed spectacles with heavy black frames. He was a tall angular man dressed in chauffeur's livery. His small shaved skull merging into his wide curved nose gave him the appearance of a snapping turtle, and with the spectacles he looked as though he were trying to pass himself off as human. He might have been disagreeable but he wasn't stupid. He was Mister Sam's friend.

"Mister Sam," he said, "I tells you right here and now to your face — I think you is nuts. You has lost whatever sense you was born with."

Mister Sam's eyes closed to slits of milky blue in his shrunken face. "Folks don't know everything," he whispered.

"I helps the old and the sick," Doctor Mubuta jawed. "I rejuvenates the disrejuvenated."

"Shit! Get yo'self in hand, Mister Sam. Look yo' life in the face. Here you is ninety years old. . . . "

"More than that."

"More than ninety, with almost all of yo'self in the grave, been diddling all kinds of women for sixty-five years."

"Longer than that."

"Been pimping and running whore house ever since you learned the stuff would sell —"

"Jes business. Buy low and sell high. It's Jewish."

"Been surrounded with women all yo' life, and ain't satisfied yet. Here you is nearmost a hundred years old and wants to go against the ordained order of creation."

"Tain't dat!"

"Tain't dat!" Johnson X controlled himself. "Mister Sam, does you believe in God?"

"Dat's it. I been believing in God for sixty-nine years. That's 'fore you was born."

Johnson X looked stumped. "Come again, I don't dig you."

"God helps them who helps themselves."

Johnson X's eyes popped, his voice became outraged. "Old and wicked as you is, as much sin as you has sinned in yo' life, as many people as you has cheated, all the lies you has told, all the stuff you has stole, you means to lie there and say you is expecting some help from God?"

"Nothing takes the place of God," Doctor Mubuta said in his

singsong voice, sounding as pious as possible, then added as an afterthought, as though he might have gone too far, "but money."

"Pick up that there Gladstone bag," Mister Sam croaked.

Doctor Mubuta lifted the Gladstone bag that sat on the floor beside his doctor's bag.

"Look in it," Mister Sam ordered.

Doctor Mubuta opened the bag dutifully and looked into it, and for the first time his expression changed and his eyes seemed about to pop from his head.

"What you see?" Mister Sam urged.

"Money," Doctor Mubuta whispered.

"You think that's enough money to take the place of God?"

"Looks like it. Looks like an awful lot to me."

"It's all I got."

Van Raff stood up. Viola turned bright red.

"And it's yours," Mister Sam informed Doctor Mubuta.

"No, it isn't," Van Raff shouted.

"I'se going for the police," Johnson X said.

"Sit down," Mister Sam croaked evilly. "Jes testing y'all. Ain't nothing but paper."

Doctor Mubuta's face closed like the Bible.

"Let me see it," Van Raff demanded.

"Is I is or is I ain't?" Doctor Mubuta demanded.

"I think someone ought to stop this," Anny said apologetically. "I don't think it's right."

"Tend to your own business," her husband snarled.

"Excuse me for living," she replied, giving him a furious look.

"He ought to be put in the 'sylum," Viola said. "He's crazy."

"I'm going to look at it," Van Raff declared, moving forward to take the bag.

"And I found y'all out," Mister Sam said.

"Now you've all had your say, can I proceed with the procedure?" Doctor Mubuta said.

"Leave it be," Johnson X said to Van Raff. "It ain't going nowhere."

"It sure ain't," Van Raff declared, sullenly returning to his seat.

Neither of the teen-age girls had spoken.

In the strained silence, Doctor Mubuta opened his bag and extracted a quart-size jar containing a nasty-looking liquid and placed it atop the bed table beside Mister Sam's bed. Everyone leaned forward to stare incredulously at the milky liquid.

Mister Sam stretched his neck and popped his old glazed eyes like a curious old rooster with a bare neck.

"Is that the stuff?"

"That's the stuff."

"Gonna make me young?"

"That's what it's for."

"What's that milky stuff floating around in it?"

"That's albumin. The same stuff as is the base for semen."

"What's semen?"

"What you ain't got."

All of a sudden the teen-aged white girl became hysterical. She doubled over laughing and choking and her face turned bright red. Everyone stared at her until she got over it, then turned their attention back to the jar of rejuvenating liquid.

"What's them black balls floating around?" Mister Sam asked.

"Just what they look like, black balls, only they is taken from a baboon, which is the most virile two-footed animal known."

Mister Sam's lids flickered. "You don't say. Taken from a live baboon?"

"Live when they was took, and rearing to go."

"Ain't that sompin. Bet he didn't like it."

"No more than you would'ave fifty years ago."

"Uhm! And what's them things that looks like feathers?"

"They is feathers. Rooster primaries. From a fighting rooster what could fertilize eggs from a distance of three feet."

"Reminds me of a man I knew what could look at womens and knock 'em up."

"He had a concupiscent eye. One of them is in there too."

"You ain't missed nothing, is you? Balls and feathers and eyes and summon. What's all them other strange-looking things?"

"All of them is mating organs of rabbits, eagles and shellfish."

Doctor Mubuta uttered these pronouncements without the flicker of an eyelash. His audience stared at him with their eyes popping out. Within the frame of reference — light, heat and Harlem — at some time during the recitation they had all passed the line of rational rejection. It wasn't hard. It wasn't any harder to believe in rejuvenation than to believe equality was coming.

"You sho' got some mixture there, if they all start working at the same time, I'll say that much," Mister Sam conceded admiringly. "But what's that black slimy stuff at the bottom?"

"That's the secret," Doctor Mubuta replied, as solemn as an owl.

"Oh, that's the secret, eh? Looks like hog shit to me."

"That's the stuff which invigorates the other stuff which charges the genital glands, like charging a rundown battery."

"Is that what it does?"

"That's what it does."

"What's it called?"

"Sperm elixir."

"Sounds mighty fancy. You sure it gonna work?"

Doctor Mubuta looked down at Mister Sam contemptuously. "If you didn't know this elixir would work, you wouldn't have me here giving you none, cheap and stingy as you is."

"All I know is what I've heard," Mister Sam admitted grudgingly.

"What you has heard," Doctor Mubuta said scornfully. "You has seen people it has worked on. You has been sneaking around asking questions and spying on my clients ever since I have been back from Africa."

Johnson X was indignant. "I'm ashamed of you, Mister Sam. Ashamed! You used to have the reputation of being a real big sport, you enjoyed your pleasure and didn't grudge nobody. And now here you is, sitting on a fortune you has made from the sinning of others, and you is so envious of the pleasures of others you is gonna give all yo' money to be able to sin again yo'self — and it ain't really yo' own money, as old as you is."

"Ain't that," Mister Sam protested. "I wants to get married again."

"Ise his fiancy," the teen-aged white girl said. Her flat unemotional announcement, spoken in a jarring voice straight out of the cotton fields of the South, exploded in the room like a hand grenade, causing far more repercussions than the exposing of the rejuvenating elixir.

So much blood rushed to Viola's head it looked like a gorged bedbug. "You beast," she screamed. Which one she meant, no one knew.

"Don't worry, he can't do nothing," Van Raff consoled her, trying to shake down the blood in his own head.

But it was Anny who looked so ashamed. Noticing, Dick said harshly, "He gonna be young, ain't he? Don't go back on your race now!"

And for an instant the mask slipped from Doctor Mubuta's face and he looked more stupid than ever. "Huh! You going to marry this here, uh, young missy?"

"What's the matter with her?" Mister Sam asked challengingly.

"Matter with her! Ain't nothing the matter with her — it's you I is thinking about. You is going to need more of this here elixir than I has figured."

"You think I ain't thought of that."

"And what is more," Doctor Mubuta went on. "If I heard you correctly, and if what is common knowledge all over Harlem is the truth, you already has one wife, who is here present in this here room and two wives is too many for this elixir at yo' age."

"Give her some too, so she be young as me, and can peddle her pussy."

The teen-age white girl became hysterical again.

Viola popped open a switchblade knife from her purse and charged the girl. Van Raff was caught by surprise and couldn't move. The white girl ran behind Mister Sam's bed as though he could help her. Viola changed directions and headed toward Mister Sam with the open blade. Doctor Mubuta clutched her about the waist. Johnson X started forward. Van Raff jumped to his feet. Viola was trying to stab Doctor Mubuta and his hand was getting slashed as he grabbed for the knife.

He was reaching for the Gladstone when Van Raff came up from behind, shouting, "Oh, no, you don't!" and snatched it out of his hand. Simultaneously Viola stabbed him in the back. It wasn't enough to hamper him and he wheeled on her in a red-eyed rage and clutched the blade with his bleeding hand as though it were an icicle, and jerked it from her hand. Her gray eyes were stretched in fear and outrage and her pink mouth opened for a scream, showing a lot of vein-laced throat. But she never got to scream. He stabbed her in the heart, and in the same motion turned and stabbed Van Raff in the head, breaking the knife blade on his skull. Van Raff looked a sudden hundred years old as his face fell apart in shock, and the Gladstone bag dropped from his nerveless fingers.

With blood coming out of his back and hand as though his arteries were leaking, Doctor Mubuta snatched up the bag and headed for the door. Dick and Anny had disappeared and Johnson X was standing in the door like a cross to keep anyone from entering. Doctor Mubuta ran up behind him and stabbed him in the back with the broken knife blade and Johnson X went out into the dining-room as though a rocket booster had gone off. Doctor Mubuta left the knife in his back and made for the kitchen door. The door opened from the outside and a short muscular black man in a red fez came in. The man had an open knife with a six-inch blade in his hand. Doctor Mubuta drew up short. But it didn't help him. The short muscular man handled his knife with authority and stabbed Doctor Mubuta to death before he could utter a sound.

6

The speaker standing on an upturned barrel at the intersection of 135th Street and Seventh Avenue was shouting monotonously: "BLACK POWER! BLACK POWER! Is you is? Or is you ain't? We gonna march this night! March! March! March! *Oh, when the saints* — yeah, baby! We gonna march this night!"

Spit flew from his looselipped mouth. His flabby jowls flopped up and down. His rough brown skin was greasy with sweat. His dull red eyes looked tired.

"Mistah Charley been scared of BLACK POWER since the day one. That's why Noah shuffled us off to Africa the time of the flood. And all this time we been laughing to keep from whaling."

He mopped his sweating face with a red bandanna handkerchief. He belched and swallowed. His eyes looked vacant. His mouth hung open as though searching for words. "Can't keep this up," he said under his breath. No one heard him. No one noticed his behavior. No one cared.

He swallowed loudly and screamed. "TONIGHT'S THE NIGHT! We launch our whale boats. Iss the night of the great white whale. You dig me, baby?"

He was a big man and flabby all over like his jowls. Night had fallen but the black night air was as hot as the bright day air, only there was less of it. His white short-sleeved shirt was sopping wet. A ring of sweat had formed about the waist of his black alpaca pants as though the top of his potbelly had begun to melt.

"You want a good house? You got to whale! You want a good car? You got to whale! You want a good job? You got to whale! You dig me?"

His conked hair was dripping sweat. For a big flabby middle-aged man who would have looked more at home in a stud poker game, he was unbelievably hysterical. He waved his arms like an erratic windmill. He cut a dance step. He shuffled like a prizefighter. He shadowed with clenched fists. He shouted. Spit flew. "Whale! Whale! WHALE, WHITEY! WE GOT THE POWER! WE IS BLACK! WE IS PURE!"

A crowd of Harlem citizens dressed in holiday garb had assembled to listen. They crowded across the sidewalks, into the street, blocking traffic. They were clad in the chaotic colors of a South American jungle. They could have been flowers growing on the banks of the Amazon, wild orchids of all colors. Except for their voices.

"What's he talking 'bout?" a high-yellow chick with bright red hair wearing a bright green dress that came down just below her buttocks asked the tall slim black man with smooth carved features and etched hair.

"Hush yo' mouth an' lissen," he replied harshly, giving her a furious look from the corners of muddy, almond-shaped eyes. "He tellin' us what black power mean!"

She opened her big green eyes speckled with brown tints and looked at him in astonishment.

"Black power? It don't mean nothing to me. I ain't black."

His carved lips curled in scorn. "Whose fault is that?"

"BLACK POWER IS MIGHTY! GIVE FOR THE FIGHT!"

When the comely young brownskinned miss presented her collection basket to a group of sports of all sorts in front of the Paradise Inn, repeating in her soft, pleasant voice: "Give for the fight, gentlemen," one conk-haired joker in a long-sleeved red silk shirt said offensively, "What mother-raping fight? If Black Power all that powerful, who needs to fight? It ought to be giving me something."

She looked the sports up and down, unperturbed. "Go back to your white tramps; we black women are going to fight."

"Well, go 'head and fight then," the sport said, turning away. "That's what's wrong with you black women, you fights too much."

But some of the other young women collecting for the fight were more successful. For among the holiday-makers there were many serious persons who understood the necessity for a fund for the coming fight. They believed in Black Power. They'd give it a trial anyway. Everything else had failed. They filled the collection baskets with coins and bills. It was going anyway, for one thing and another. Rent, religion, food or whiskey, why not for Black Power? What did they have to lose? And they might win. Who knew? The whale swallowed Jonah. Moses split the Red Sea. Christ rose from the dead. Lincoln freed the slaves. Hitler killed six million Jews. The Africans had got to rule — in some parts of Africa, anyway. The Americans and the Russians have shot the moon. Some joker has made a plastic heart. Anything is possible.

The young ladies dumped their filled baskets into a gilt-painted keg with the banner BLACK POWER on a low table to one side of the speaker's barrel, presided over by a buxom, stern-faced, gray-haired matron clad in a black dress uniform lit up with gilt buttons and masses of braid who looked like an effigy beginning to burn on that hot day. And then they went back into the crowd to fill them again.

The speaker raved: "BLACK POWER! DANGEROUS AS THE DARK! MYSTERIOUS AS THE NIGHT! Our heritage! Our birthright! Unchain us in the big cor-ral!"

"Joker sounds like he's shooting craps," one brother whispered to another.

The few white motorists threading their way through the crowd, going north on Seventh Avenue in the direction of Westchester County, looked curiously at the crowd, opened their windows and heard the words, "BLACK POWER," and stepped on the gas.

It was an orderly crowd. Police cars lined the streets. But the cops had nothing to do except avoid the challenging stares. Most of the patrol-car cops were white, but they had become slightly reddened under the hysterical ranting of the speaker and the monotonous repetition of "BLACK POWER".

A black Cadillac limousine, shining in the sun like polished jet, whispered to the curb in the no-parking zone for the crosstown bus stop, within touching distance of the orator's barrel. Two dangerous-looking black men clad in black leather coats and what looked like officers' caps in a Black Power army sat in the front seat, immobile, staring straight ahead with not a muscle twitching in their lumpy scarred faces. On the back seat sat a portly gray-haired black man between two slender, sedate, clean-cut brownskinned young men dressed as clerics. The gray-haired man had smooth black velvety skin that looked recently massaged. Despite his short-cropped gray kinky hair, his light-brown eyes beneath thick glossy black eyebrows were startlingly clear and youthful. Long black eyelashes gave him a sexy look. But there was nothing lush about his appearance, still less about his demeanour. He was dressed in dark gray summer worsted, black shoes, dark tie, white shirt, and wore no jewelry of any sort, not even a watch. His manner was calm, authoritative, his eyes twinkled with good humor but his mouth was firm and his face grave.

The leather-coated flunky next to the chauffeur jumped to the curb and held open the back door. The cleric on the inside stepped to the pavement, the gray-haired man followed him.

The speaker stopped abruptly in the middle of a sentence and descended from his barrel. He approached the gray-haired man with a diffidence that didn't become the masterful exhorter of Black Power. He made no attempt to shake his hand. "Doctor Moore, I need a relief," he blurted. "I'm beat."

"Carry on, J," Doctor Moore commanded. "I'll send L to relieve you shortly." His voice was modulated, his enunciation perfect, his manner pleasant, but it held an authority that brooked no contradiction.

"I'm awfully tired," J whined.

Doctor Moore gave him a sharp look, then he softened and patted his shoulder. "We are all tired, son, carry on just a little longer and you will be relieved. If just one more soul," he added, shaking his finger to emphasize his point, "gets the message our labors will not be in vain."

"Yes, sir," J said meekly and hefted his wet flabby belly back on to his barrel.

"And now, Sister Z, what have you for the cause?" Doctor Moore asked the buxom black-uniformed matron presiding over the gilt keg of BLACK POWER.

She grinned a smile of pure gold; it was like seeing Mona Lisa break into a laugh. "The keg is most near filled," she said proudly, rows of gold teeth, uppers and lowers, flashing in the light.

Doctor Moore looked at her teeth regretfully, then nodded to the cleric, who opened the trunk of the car and undid a large leather suitcase. The leather-coated flunky took the keg of money and dumped it into the suitcase, which was already half-filled with similar coins and bills.

The onlookers watched this operation in a petrified silence. From down the street the white cops in front of the 135th Street precinct station looked on curiously but didn't move. None took notice that the limousine was parked illegally. No one challenged

Doctor Moore's authority to collect the money. No one seemed to think there was anything strange about the entire procedure. But yet there were many black people among the crowd and most of the white cops in the police cars who didn't know who Doctor Moore was, who had never seen him or even heard of him. He had such a positive air of authority it seemed logical that he would collect the money, and it was taken for granted that a black Cadillac limousine filled with uniformed black people, even though two of the uniforms were clerical, was connected with Black Power.

When they had taken their respective seats again, Doctor Moore spoke into the speaking-tube, "Drive to the Center, B," then as he glanced at the back of the chauffeur's head, corrected himself: "I believe you're C, aren't you?"

The front seat wasn't partitioned off and the chauffeur turned his head slightly and said, "Yes, sir, B's dead."

"Dead? Since when?" Doctor Moore sounded mildly surprised.

"It's more than two months now."

Doctor Moore leaned back against the cushions and sighed. "Life is fleeting," he observed sadly.

Nothing more was said until they arrived at their destination. It was a middle-class housing development on upper Lenox Avenue, a large U-shaped red-brick apartment building seventeen storeys high. The front garden was so new the grass hadn't sprouted and the freshly planted trees and shrubbery looked withered as from a drought. There was a children's playground in its center with the slides and seesaws and sand-boxes so new they looked abandoned, as though no children lived there.

Across Lenox Avenue, on the West Side, toward Seventh Avenue, were the original slums with their rat-ridden, cold water flats unchanged, the dirty glass-fronted ground floors occupied by the customary supermarkets with hand-lettered ads on their plate-glass windows reading: "Fully cooked U.S. Govt. Inspected SMOKED HAMS 55c lb.... Secret Deodorant ICE-BLUE 79c.... California Seedless GRAPES 2 lbs 49c.... Fluffy ALL Controlled Suds 3 lbs pkg. 77c.... KING CRAB CLAWS lb 79c.... GLAD BAGS 99c." Delicatessens advertising: "*Frozen*

Chitterlings and other delicacies".... Notion stores with needles and buttons and thread on display.... Barbershops.... Smokeshops.... Billboards advertising: *Whiskies, beers*.... "HARYOU".... *Politicians running for Congress*.... "BEAUTY FAIR by CLAIRE: *WIGS, MEN'S HAIR PIECES, 'CAPILISCIO'* ".... Funeral Parlors.... Nightclubs.... "*Reverend Ike; 'See and hear this young man of God; A Prayer For The Sick And All Conditions in Every Service; COME WITH YOUR BURDENS LEAVE WITH A SONG'* ".... Black citizens sitting on the stoops to their cold-water flats in the broiling night.... Sports ganged in front of bars sucking marijuana.... Grit and dust and dirt and litter floating idly in the hot dense air stirred up by the passing of feet. That was the side of the slum dwellers. The ritzy residents across the street never looked their way.

The black Cadillac limousine drew to the curb in front of the unfinished lawn. Miraculously the banner across the back which had previously proclaimed BLACK POWER now read: BROTHERHOOD. The two black-coated, black-capped men in front got out first and stood flanking the rear door. Away from the motley crowd at 135th Street and Seventh Avenue, with that quiet, pretentious apartment building in the background, they looked larger, tougher, infinitely more dangerous. The bulges beneath their leather coats on the left sides were more pronounced. There, on the quiet, shady side of the old, wide, historic slum street, they looked unmistakably like bodyguards. The well-dressed people coming and going from and to the apartment entrance gave them a wide berth. But no resentment was shown. They were familiar. Doctor Moore was a noted personage. The residents held him in high esteem. They admired his efforts at integration; they commended his nonviolent, reasonable approach. When Doctor Moore himself alighted, standing between his two clerics, passing residents tipped their hats and smiled obsequiously.

"You boys come with me," he said.

He walked briskly into the building with his retinue at his heels. There were both confidence and authority in his bearing, like that of a man with a purpose and a will to achieve it. Residents passing through the foyer bowed. He smiled amiably but didn't speak. The doorman kept an empty elevator waiting for him. He rode it to the third floor, where he dismissed his bodyguards and took his clerics inside.

The entrance hall was sumptuously furnished. A wall-to-wall carpet of a dark purple color covered the floor. On one side was a coat-rack with a full-length mirror attached and beside it an umbrella stand. On the other side a long low table for hats, with twin shaded lamps at each end, flanked by straight-backed chairs of some dark exotic wood with overstuffed needlepoint seats. But Doctor Moore did not linger there. After a brief glance into the mirror he turned right into the salon along the front of the building with two wide windows, followed by his clerics. Except for translucent curtains and purple silk drapes behind white venetian blinds, the salon was as bare as Mother Hubbard's Cupboard. But Doctor Moore kept on through to the dining-room with his clerics at his heels. It was equally bare as the salon with similar blinds and curtains. But Doctor Moore did not hesitate, nor did his clerics expect him to hesitate. Into the kitchen they marched in single file. Not a word had been spoken. And as yet still without speech, his clerics shed their coats and clerical collars and donned white cotton jackets and cooks' caps while Doctor Moore peered into the refrigerator.

"They're some neckbones here," Doctor Moore said."Make some neckbones and rice and you'll find some yellow yams somewhere and maybe there's some of those collards left."

"What about some corn bread, Al?" one of the cook-clerics said.

"All right then, some corn bread, if there's any butter."

"There's some margarine."

Doctor Moore gave a grimace of distaste. "Tap the trunk," he said "A man's got to eat."

He went quickly back into the hall and opened the door to the first bedroom. It was empty except for an unmade double bed and an unpainted wardrobe.

"Lucy!" he called.

A woman stuck her head out of the bath. It was the head of a young woman with a smooth brownskinned face and straightened black hair pulled aslant her forehead over her right ear. It was a beautiful face with a wide straight nose and unflared nostrils above a wide, thick, unpainted mouth with brown lips that looked soft and resilient. Brown eyes magnified by rimless spectacles gave her a sexy look.

"Lucy's out; it's me," she said.

"You? Barbara! Somebody with you?"his voice came out in a whisper.

"Shit, naw, do you think I'd bring 'em here?" she said in a softly modulated voice which jarred shockingly with the words.

"Well, what the fuck are you doing here?" he said in a loud coarse voice that made him sound like another man altogether. "I sent you to work the cocktail party at the Americana."

She came into the room with the waft of woman smell. Her voluptuous brown body was covered loosely by a pink silk robe which showed a line of brown belly and a black growth of pubic hair.

"I was there," she said defensively. "There was too much competition from the high-society amateurs. All those hincty bitches fell on those whitey-babies like they was sugar candy."

Doctor Moore frowned angrily. "So what? Can't you out-project those amateurs? You're a pro."

"Are you kidding? Against all those free matrons? You ever see Madame Thomasina with a hot on for whitey?"

"Listen, whore, that's your problem. I don't pay to send you to these cocktail parties to let these high-society bitches beat you at the game. I expect you to score. How you do it is your business. If you can't collar a whitey John with them all about, I'll get myself another whore."

She went up to him so he could smell her and feel the woman coming from her body. "Don't talk to me like that, Al baby. Ain't I been good all along? It's just these matinees when these bitches are free. I'm sure I'll score tonight." She tried to embrace him but he pushed her away roughly.

"You better, girl," he said. "I mean business. The rent isn't paid, and I'm behind with my Caddy."

"Ain't your own pitch paying nothing?"

"Peanuts. It's split too mother-raping thin. And these Harlem folks ain't serious. All they want to do is boogaloo." He paused and then said reflectively, "I could make a mint if I could just get them mad."

"Jesus, can't your apes do that? What you got them for then?"

"No. They're useless in an operation like this," he said meditatively. "What I really need is a dead man."

7

The assistant Medical Examiner looked like a City College student in a soiled seersucker suit. His thick brown hair needed cutting and his hornrimmed glasses needed wiping. He looked as humorless as befits a man whose business is the dead.

He straightened up from examining the body and wiped his hands on his trousers. "This was an easy one," he said, addressing himself to the sergeant from the homicide bureau. "You got the exact time of death from these local men, they saw him die. The exact cause is a cut jugular vein. Male, white and approximately thirty-five years old."

The homicide sergeant wasn't satisfied with such a small capsule. He looked as though he was never satisfied with Medical Examiners. He was a thin, tall, angular man wearing what looked like a starched blue serge suit. He had reddish hair of the most repulsive shade, big brown freckles that looked like a bowl full of warts, and a long sharp nose that stuck out from his face like the keel of a racing yacht. His close-set, small blue eyes looked frustrated.

"Identifying marks? Scars? Birthmarks?"

"Hell, you saw as much as I did," the assistant M.E. said, accidentally stepping into the pool of blood. "Son of a Goddam bitch!" he cried.

"Jesus Christ, there's not a thing on him to tell who he is," the sergeant complained. "No papers, no wallet, no laundry mark on this one garment it's wearing —"

"How 'bout the shoes?" Coffin Ed ventured.

"Marked shoes?"

"Why not?"

The assistant D.A. gave him a slight nod, whatever it meant. He was a middle-aged man with a white unhealthy look and meticulously combed graying hair. His doughy face and abrupt paunch along with his wrinkled suit and unshined shoes gave him the look of a complete failure. Gathered about him were the ambulance drivers and vacant-faced patrol-car cops as though seeking shelter of his indecision. The homicide sergeant and the assistant M.E. stood apart.

The sergeant looked at the photographer he had brought with him. "Take off his shoes," he ordered.

The photographer bridled. "Let Joe take 'em off," he said. "All I take is pictures."

Joe was the detective first grade who drove for the sergeant. He was a square-built Slav with crew-cut hair that bristled like porcupine quills.

"All right, Joe," the sergeant said.

Wordlessly Joe knelt on the dirty pavement, unlaced the dead man's brown suede oxfords and drew them from his feet, one after another. He held them to the light and looked inside. The sergeant bent to look into them too.

"*Bostonian*," Joe read.

"Hell," the sergeant said disgustedly, giving Coffin Ed an appraising look. Then he turned back to the assistant M.E. with a long-suffering manner. "Can you tell me if he's had sexual intercourse — recently, I mean?"

The assistant M.E. looked bored with it all. "We can tell by the autopsy whether he's had sexual intercourse up to within an hour of death." Sotto voce, he added, "What a question."

The sergeant heard him. "It's important," he said defensively. "We got to know something about this man. How the hell we going to find out who killed him?"

"You can take his prints, of course," Coffin Ed said.

The sergeant looked at him with narrowed eyes, as though suspecting him of needling. Of course they were going to take the body's fingerprints and all other Bertillon measurements needed in identification, as the detective well knew, he thought angrily.

"Anyway, it wasn't with a woman," the assistant M.E. said, reddening uncontrollably. "At least in a normal way."

Everyone looked at him, as though expecting him to say more.

"Right," the sergeant concurred, nodding knowingly. But he would have liked to ask the assistant M.E. how he knew.

Then suddenly Grave Digger said, "I could have told you that from the start."

The sergeant reddened so furiously his freckles stood out like scars. He had heard of these two colored detectives up here, but this was the first time he had seen them. But he could already tell that a little bit of them went a long way; in other words, they were getting on his ass.

"Then maybe you can tell me why he was killed, too," he said sarcastically.

"That's easy," Grave Digger said with a straight face. "There are only two reasons a white man is killed in Harlem. Money or fear."

The sergeant wasn't expecting that answer. It threw him. He lost his sarcasm. "Not sex?"

"Sex? Hell, that's all you white people can think of, Harlem and sex — and you're right, too!" he went on before the sergeant could speak. "You'r right as rain. But sex is for sale. And all the surplus they give away. So why kill a white sucker for that? That's killing the goose that lays the golden egg."

Color drained from the sergeant's face and it became white from anger. "Are you trying to tell me there are no sex murders here?"

"What I said was there were no white men killed for sex," Grave Digger said equably. "Ain't no white man ever that involved."

Color flowed back into the sergeant's face, which was changing color under his guilt complexes like a chameleon. "And no one ever makes a mistake?" He felt compelled to argue just for the sake of arguing.

"Hell, sergeant, every murder's a mistake," Grave Digger said condescendingly. "You know that, it's your business."

Yes, these black sons of bitches were going to take a lot of getting along with, the sergeant thought, as he grimly changed the conversation.

"Well, maybe I should have asked do you know who killed him?"

"That ain't fair," Coffin Ed said roughly.

The sergeant threw up his hands. "I give up."

Including the patrol-car cops, most of whom were white, there were fifteen white officers gathered about the body, and in addition to Grave Digger and Coffin Ed, four colored patrol-car cops. All laughed from relief. It was a touchy business when a white man was killed in Harlem. People took up sides on racial lines, regardless of whether they were police officers or not. No one liked it, but all were involved. It was personal to them all.

"Anything else you want to know?" the assistant M.E. asked.

The sergeant looked at him sharply to see if he was being sarcastic. He decided he was innocent. "Yeah, everything," he replied, waxing loquacious. "Who he is? Who killed him? Why? Most of all I want the killer. That's my job."

"That's your baby," the assistant M.E. said. "By tomorrow — or rather this morning — we'll give you the physiological details. Right now I'm going home." He filled out a DOA tag, which he tied to the right big toe of the body, and nodded to the drivers of the police hearse. "Take it to the morgue."

The homicide sergeant stood absently watching the body loaded, then looked slowly about from the idle car cops to the congregated black people. "All right, boys," he ordered. "Take them all in."

The homicide department always took over investigations of homicide and the highest ranking homicide detective on the scene became the boss. Detectives from the local precinct and patrol-car cops who took instructions either from the precinct captain or a divisional inspector didn't always like this arrangement. But

Grave Digger and Coffin Ed didn't care who became boss. "We just get pissed-off with all the red tape," Grave Digger once said. "We want to get down to the nitty-gritty."

But there were formalities to protect the rights of citizens and they couldn't just light into a group of innocent people and start whipping head until somebody talked, which they figured was the best and cheapest way to solve a crime. If the citizens didn't like it, they ought to stay at home. Since they couldn't do this, they began to walk away.

"Come on," Coffin Ed urged. "This man will have us picked up next."

"Look at these brothers flee," Grave Digger noted. "They wouldn't listen to me when I warned them."

They went only as far as the littered paved square strewed with overflowing garbage cans beside the front stairs to the nearest rooming house where they could watch the operation without being seen. The smell of rotting garbage was nauseating.

"Whew! Who said us colored people were starving?"

"That ain't what they say, Digger. They just wonder why we ain't."

As the first of the onlookers were loaded in the police wagon, other curious citizens arrived.

"Whuss happening?"

"Search me, baby. Some whitey was killed, they say."

"Shot?"

"Washed away."

"They got who done it?"

"You kidding? They just grabbing off us folks. You know how white cops is."

"Less split."

"Too late," said a white car cop who thought he dug the soul brother, taking each by the arm.

"He thinks he's funny," one of the brothers complained.

"Well, ain't he?" the other admitted, looking expressively at their arms in his grip.

"Joe, you and Ted bright the power lamps," the sergeant called above the hubbub. "Looks like there's a blood trail here."

Followed by his assistants with the battery-powered spot lamps, the sergeant stepped down into the garbage-scented courtyard. "I'll need you men's help," he said. "There must be a blood trail here." He had decided to adopt a conciliatory manner.

People gathered on the adjoining rooming-house steps, trying to see what they were doing. A patrol car drew to the curb, the two uniformed cops in the front seat looking on with interest.

The sergeant became exasperated. "You officers get these people out the way," he ordered irritably.

The cops got sullen. "Hey, you folks get over there with the others," one ordered.

"I lives here," a buxom light-complexioned woman wearing gilt mules and a stained blue nightgown muttered defiantly. "I just got out of bed to see what the noise was all about."

"Now you know," the homicide photographer said slyly.

The woman grinned gratefully.

"Do as you're ordered!" the car cop shouted angrily, stepping to the sidewalk.

The woman's plaits shook in outrage. "Who you talking to?" she shouted back. "You can't order me off my own steps."

"You tell 'em sister Berry," a pajama-clad brother behind her encouraged.

The cop was getting red. The other cop climbed from beneath the wheel on the other side and came around the car threateningly. "What was that you said?" he challenged.

She looked toward Grave Digger and Coffin Ed for support.

"Don't look at me," Grave Digger said. "I'm the law too."

"That's a nigger for you," the woman said scornfully as the white cops marched them off.

"All right, now bring the light here," the sergeant said, returning to the dark purple pool of congealing blood where the murdered man had died.

Before joining the others, Grave Digger went back to their car and turned off the lights.

The trail wasn't hard to follow. It had a pattern. An irregular patch of scattered spots that looked like spots of tar in the artificial light was interspersed every fourth or fifth step by a dark gleaming splash where blood had spurted from the wound. Now that all the soul people had been removed from the street, the five detectives moved swiftly. But they could still feel the presence of teeming people behind the dilapidated stone façades of the old reconverted buildings. Here and there the white gleams of eyes showed from darkened windows, but the silence was eerie.

The trail turned from the sidewalk into an unlighted alleyway between the house beyond the rooming house, which described itself by a sign in a front window reading: *Kitchenette Apts. All conveniences*, and the weather-streaked red-brick apartment beyond that. The alleyway was so narrow they had to go in single file. The sergeant had taken the power light from his driver, Joe, and was leading the way himself. The pavement slanted down sharply beneath his feet and he almost lost his step. Midway down the blank side of the building he came to a green wooden door. Before touching it, he flashed his light along the sides of the flanking buildings. There were windows in the kitchenette apartments, but all from the top to the bottom floor had folding iron grilles which were closed and locked at that time of night, and dark shades were drawn on all but three. The apartment house had a vertical row of small black openings one above the other at the rear. They might have been bathroom windows but no light showed in any of them and the glass was so dirty it didn't shine.

The blood trail ended at the green door.

"Come out of there," the sergeant said.

No one answered.

He turned the knob and pushed the door and it opened inward so silently and easily he almost fell into the opening before he could train his light. Inside was a black dark void.

Grave Digger and Coffin Ed flattened themselves against the walls on each side of the alley and their big long-barreled .38 revolvers came glinting into their hands.

"What the hell!" the sergeant exclaimed, startled.

His assistants ducked.

"This is Harlem," Coffin Ed grated and Grave Digger elaborated:

"We don't trust doors that open."

Ignoring them, the sergeant shone his light into the opening. Crumbling brick stairs went down sharply to a green iron grille.

"Just a boiler room," the sergeant said and put his shoulders through the doorway. "Hey, anybody down there?" he called. Silence greeted him.

"You go down, Joe, I'll light your way," the sergeant said.

"Why me?" Joe protested.

"Me and Digger'll go," Coffin Ed said. "Ain't nobody there who's alive."

"I'll go myself," the sergeant said tersely. He was getting annoyed.

The stairway went down underneath the ground floor to a depth of about eight feet. A short paved corridor ran in front of the boiler room at right angles to the stairs, where each end was closed off by unpainted panelled doors. Both the stairs and the corridor felt like loose gravel underfoot, but otherwise they were clean. Splotches of blood were more in evidence in the corridor and a bloody hand mark showed clearly on the unpainted door to the rear.

"Let's not touch anything," the sergeant cautioned, taking out a clean white handkerchief to handle the doorknob.

"I better call the fingerprint crew," the photographer said.

"No, Joe will call them; I'll need you. And you local fellows better wait outside, we're so crowded in here we'll destroy the evidence."

"Ed and I won't move," Grave Digger said.

Coffin Ed grunted.

Taking no further notice of them, the sergeant pushed open the door. It was black and dark inside. First he shone his light over the wall alongside the door and all over the corridor looking for electric light switches. One was located to the right of each door. Taking care to avoid stepping in any of the blood splotches, the sergeant moved from one switch to another, but none worked. "Blown fuse," he muttered, picking his way back to the open room.

Without having to move, Grave Digger and Coffin Ed could see all they wanted through the open door. Originally made to accommodate a part-time janitor or any type of laborer who would fire the boiler for a place to sleep, the room had been converted into a pad. All that remained of the original was a partitioned-off toilet in one corner and a washbasin in the other. An opening enclosed by heavy wire mesh opened into the boiler room, serving for both ventilation and heat. Otherwise the room was furnished like a boudoir. There was a dressing-table with a triple mirror, three-quarter bed with chenille spread, numerous foam-rubber pillows in a variety of shapes, three round yellow scatter rugs. On the whitewashed walls an obscene mural had been painted in watercolors depicting black and white silhouettes in a variety of perverted sex acts, some of which could only be performed by male contortionists. And everything was splattered with blood, the walls, the bed, the rugs. The furnishings were not so much disarrayed, as though a violent struggle had taken place, but just bloodied.

"Mother-raper stood still and let his throat be cut," Grave Digger observed.

"Wasn't that," Coffin Ed corrected. "He just didn't believe it is all."

The photographer was taking pictures with a small pocket camera but the sergeant sent him back to the car for his big Bertillon camera. Grave Digger and Coffin Ed left the cellar to look around.

The apartment was only one room wide but four storeys high. The front was flush with the sidewalk, and the front entrance elevated by two recessed steps. The alleyway at the side slanted down from the sidewalk sufficiently to drop the level of the door six feet below the ground-floor level. The cellar, which could only be entered by the door at the side, was directly below the ground-floor rooms. There were no apartments. Each of the four floors had three bedrooms opening on to the public hall, and to the rear was a kitchen and a bath and a separate toilet to serve each floor. There were three tenants on each floor, their doors secured by hasps and staples to be padlocked when they were absent, bolts and chains and floor locks and angle bars to protect them from intruders when they were present. The doors were pitted and scarred either because of lost keys or attempted burglary, indicating a continuous warfare between the residents and enemies from without, rapists, robbers, homicidal husbands and lovers, or the landlord after his rent. The walls were covered with obscene graffiti, mammoth sexual organs, vulgar limericks, opened legs, telephone numbers, outright boasting, insidious suggestions, and impertinent or pertinent comments about various tenants' love habits, their mothers and fathers, the legitimacy of their children.

"And people live here," Grave Digger said, his eyes sad.

"That's what it was made for."

"Like maggots in rotten meat."

"It's rotten enough."

Twelve mailboxes were nailed to the wall in the front hall. Narrow stairs climbed to the top floor. The ground-floor hallway ran through a small back courtyard where four overflowing garbage cans leaned against the wall.

"Anybody can come in here day or night," Grave Digger said. "Good for the whores but hard on the children."

"I wouldn't want to live here if I had any enemies," Coffin Ed said. "I'd be scared to go to the john."

"Yeah, but you'd have central heating."

"Personally, I'd rather live in the cellar. It's private with its own private entrance and I could control the heat."

"But you'd have to put out the garbage cans," Grave Digger said.

"Whoever occupied that whore's crib ain't been putting out any garbage cans."

"Well, let's wake up the brothers on the ground floor."

"If they ain't already awake."

8

"You're assuming that I'm a criminal because I'm married to a Negro and living in a Negro neighbourhood," Anny said tremulously. She still wore the dazed look from too much nigger and too much blood and the two black detectives weren't helping it any. She was down in the pigeon's nest on the bolted stool with the bright lights pouring over her, like any other suspect, but she'd already had a taste of this eye-searing glare and that didn't bother her as much as the indignity.

Coffin Ed and Grave Digger stood back in the shadow beyond the perimeter of the glare and she couldn't see their expressions.

"How does it feel?" Grave Digger asked.

"I know what you mean," she said. "I've always said it was unfair."

"We're holding you as a material witness," he explained.

"It's after midnight now," Coffin Ed said. "By eight o'clock this morning you'll be sprung."

"What he means is we've got to get such information as we can before then," Grave Digger explained.

"I don't know much," she said. "My husband's the one you ought to question."

"We'll get to him, we got to you," Coffin Ed said.

"It all came from Mister Sam wanting to get rejuvenated," she said.

"Did you believe in that?" Grave Digger asked.

"You sound like his chauffeur, Johnson X," she said.

He didn't dispute her.

"All colored people sound alike," Coffin Ed muttered.

A slow blush crept over her pale face. "It wasn't so hard," she confessed. "It was harder for my husband. You see, I have come to believe in a lot of things most people consider unbelievable."

Grave Digger continued the questioning. "How long had you known about it?"

"A couple of weeks."

"Did Mister Sam tell you?"

"No, my husband told me."

"What did he think about it?"

"He just thought it was a trick his father was playing on his wife, Viola."

"What kind of trick?"

"To get rid of her."

"Kill her?"

"Oh, no, he just wanted to be rid of her. You see, he knew she was having an affair with his attorney, Van Raff."

"Did you know him well?"

"Not well. He considered me his son's property, and he wouldn't poach —"

"Although he wanted to?"

"Maybe, but he was so old — that's why he wanted to be rejuvenated."

"To have you?"

"Oh, no, he had his own. One white woman was the same as another to him — only younger."

"Mildred?"

"Yes , the little tramp." She didn't say it vindictively, it was just descriptive.

"Anyway, she's young enough," Coffin Ed said.

"And he figured his wife and his lawyer were after his money?" Grave Digger surmised.

"That's what started it," she said, and then suddenly, as the memory washed over her, she buried her face in her hands. "Oh, it was horrible," she sobbed. "Suddenly they were savaging one another like wild beasts."

"It's the jungle, ain't it?" Coffin Ed growled. "What did you expect?"

"The blood, the blood," she moaned. "Everyone was bleeding."

Grave Digger waited for her to regain her composure,

exchanging looks with Coffin Ed. Both were thinking maybe hers was the solution but was it the time? Would sexual integration start inside the black ghetto or outside in the white community? But it didn't seem as though she would regain her composure, so Grave Digger asked, "Who started the cutting?"

"Mister Sam's wife jumped up to attack Mister Sam's little tramp, but suddenly she turned on Doctor Mubuta. I suppose it was because of the money," she added.

"What money?"

"Mister Sam had a satchel full of money under the bed which he said he was going to give to Doctor Mubuta for making him young."

The detectives froze. More blood was shed for money in Harlem than for any other reason.

"How much?"

"He said it was all he had —"

"Have you heard about the money?" Grave Digger asked Coffin Ed.

"No. Homicide must know. We'd better check with Anderson."

"Later." He turned back to Anny. "Did everyone see it?"

"Actually it was in a Gladstone bag," Anny said. "He let Doctor Mubuta look into the bag, but didn't anyone else actually see it. But Doctor Mubuta looked like it was a lot of money —"

"Looked like?"

"His expression. He seemed surprised."

"By the money?"

"By the amount, I suppose. The attorney demanded to see it. But Mister Sam — or maybe it was Doctor Mubuta — shut the bag and put it back beneath the bed, then Mister Sam said it was just paper, that he was joking. But everything seemed to change after that, as though the air got filled with violence. Mister Sam told Doctor Mubuta to go on with the experiment — the rejuvenation — because he wanted to be young again so he could marry. Then Mister Sam's tramp — Mildred — said she was his fiancée, and Mister Sam's wife, Viola, jumped up and took a knife out of her bag and ran towards the tramp — girl — and she crawled underneath Mister Sam's bed, so Mister Sam's wife turned on Doctor Mubuta, and Mister Sam drank some rejuvenating fluid and began to howl like a dog. I'm sure Doctor Mubuta didn't expect that reaction, he seemed to turn white. But he had the presence of mind to push Mister Sam down on the bed, and shout to us to run —"

Grave Digger broke the spell of his absorbed fascination and asked, "Why?"

"Why what?"

"Why run?"

"He said the 'Bird of Youth' was entering."

Grave Digger stared at her. Coffin Ed stared at her.

"How old are you?" Coffin Ed asked.

Her mind was so locked in the terrifying memory she didn't hear the question. She didn't see them. Her vision had turned back to that terrifying moment and she looked as though she were blind. "Then when Johnson X, Mister Sam's chauffeur, began to howl too — until then he had seemed the sanest one — we ran. . . ."

"Up to your apartment?"

"And locked the door."

"And you didn't see what happened to the bag of money?"

"We didn't see anything else."

"When did Van Raff come upstairs?"

"Oh, sometime later — I don't know how long. He knocked on the door a long time before we opened it, then Dick, my husband, peeped out and found him unconscious on the floor and we brought him in —"

"Did he have the bag of money?"

"No, he had been stabbed all over the head and —"

"We know all that. Now who were all the people at this shindig?"

"There were me and Dick, my husband —"

"We know he's your husband, you don't have to keep on insisting," Coffin Ed interrupted.

She tried to see his face through the curtain of shadow and Grave Digger went over to the wall and turned the lights down.

"That better?" he asked.
"Yes, we're black cops," Coffin Ed said.
"Don't insist," she said, getting back some of her own. "I can see it."
Grave Digger chuckled. "Your husband —" he prompted.
"My husband," she repeated defiantly. "He's Mister Sam's son, you know."
"We know."
"And Mister Sam's wife, Viola, and Mister Sam's attorney, Van Raff, and Mister Sam's chauffeur, Johnson X, and Mister Sam's tramp — fiancée — Mildred —"
"What you got against her? You changed your race?" Coffin Ed interrupted.
"Leave her be," Grave Digger cautioned.
But she wasn't daunted. "Yes, but not to your race, to the human race."
"That'll hold him."
"Naw, it won't. I got no reverence for these white women going 'round joining the human race. It ain't that easy for us colored folks."
"Later, man, later," Grave Digger said. "Let's stick to our business."
"That is our business."
"All right. But let's cook one pigeon at the time."
"Why?"
"You're right," Anny said. "It's too easy for us."
"That's all I said," Coffin Ed said, and having made his point, withdrew into the shadow.
"And Doctor Mubuta," Grave Digger said, taking up where she had left off.
"Yes, of course. I haven't got anything against Mildred," she added, reverting to the question. "But when a teen-age girl like her takes up with a dirty old man like Mister Sam, just for what she can get out of him, she's a tramp, that's all."
"All right," Grave Digger conceded.
"And Sugartit," she said.
"She was the one sent to the hospital? What's her name?"

"I don't know her real name, just Sugartit."

"She was the teen-age colored girl — whycome she ain't a tramp?" Coffin Ed said.

"She just wasn't, that's all."

"I have a daughter they used to call Sugartit," he said.

"This girl's not your daughter," Anny said, looking at him. "This girl's sick."

He didn't know whether she meant it as a jibe or a compliment.

"Is she a relative of Mister Sam's?" Grave Digger asked.

"I don't think so. I don't know why she was there."

"Doctor Mubuta?"

"Maybe, I don't know. All I know about her is what people say, that she's 'covered'. It seems she's the girl friend of the Syndicate's district boss — if that's what he's called. Anyway the top man."

"How'd you get to know her?"

"I didn't really know her. She'd wander into the flat sometimes — always when Dick was out. I think it might have been when the Syndicate boss was seeing Mister Sam downstairs."

Grave Digger's head moved slowly up and down. An idea was knocking at his mind, trying to get in. He looked at Coffin Ed and saw he was disturbed by a nagging idea too. The Syndicate didn't have any business in a joke like this. If an old man with a cheating, scheming wife wanted to risk his life with a charlatan like Doctor Mubuta, that was his business. But the Syndicate wouldn't have a lookout staked unless there was more to it than that.

"And the last you saw of the Gladstone bag full of money was when Doctor Mubuta put it back underneath the bed?" he asked. Coffin Ed gave a slight nod.

"Oh, it was there all the time, when Viola rushed at Mildred and when she turned on Doctor Mubuta and it was there when he yelled for us to run —"

"Maybe the 'Bird of Youth' took it," Coffin Ed said.

"You know he was killed too — Doctor Mubuta?"

"Yes."

"Who told you?" he shot the question at her.

"Why you did," she said. "Don't you remember? When you

brought me and Dick here? You asked him were we present when the doctor was killed."

"I'd forgotten," he confessed sheepishly.

"I hated for him to be killed more than anyone," she said. "I knew he was a fake —"

"How'd you know it?"

"He had to be —"

"Earlier you said —"

"I know what I said. But he touched me."

Both of them looked at her with new interest.

"How so?" Grave Digger asked.

"When he was telling Mister Sam he'd discovered the solution for the Negro problem was for Negroes to outlive the white people."

They looked at her curiously. "You're a strange woman," Grave Digger said.

"Because I was moved by the idea?" she asked surprisedly. "I was just ashamed."

"Well, he's found the final solution now," Grave Digger said.

Next they interviewed Dick. He answered their questions with a lackadaisical indifference. He didn't seem affected by either the death of his father or his stepmother, and he couldn't care less about the others. Sure, he knew Doctor Mubuta was a con man, all the hepcats in Harlem had him made. Of course his father knew, he and Doctor Mubuta were in cahoots. They probably staged the act for Mister Sam to cache some money away. His father was senile but he wasn't a square, he knew his wife and Van Raff were teaming up on him. The way he figured it, it looked like Doctor Mubuta crossed the old man, he felt certain the Gladstone bag was filled with money. But he couldn't figure what went wrong at the end, there had to be another person.

"Who?" Grave Digger asked.

"How the hell do I know?" he answered.

He'd never had any part in Mister Sam's rackets. All he knew was his old man fronted for four numbers houses; he would appear at the houses when the tallies were made and the hits paid off. But other people ran the show. The numbers were like a Wall

Street brokerage these days. There were girls with calculators and clerks operating adding machines and a supervisor at each house directing the business. The runners collected the plays from the writers and collected the hits from the house and paid them back to the writers who paid off the players and the staffs at the houses never saw the players. In fact they were like high-paid clerks; they bought big cars and houses on credit and lived it up. His father was just a figurehead and a fall guy in case someone had to take a rap, the Syndicate was the real boss. He didn't know whether his father got a salary or a commission, anyway, he did all right for himself considering his age, but the Syndicate took forty percent of the gross.

"Good picking," Grave Digger said drily.

"Multimillion-dollar business," Dick agreed.

"Why didn't you take a cut?" Coffin Ed asked curiously.

"I'm a musician," Dick said as though that were the answer.

He didn't know anything about Sugartit, he said. He saw her the first time at the seance, if that's what you want to call it. The only way he knew her name was hearing Anny call her Sugartit.

"Does you wife know much about the Harlem scene?" Grave Digger asked.

For the first time Dick gave a question thought.

"I don't really know," he confessed. "She's at home alone a lot. Most nights she catches the show at The Spot and we go home together. But I don't know what she does with her days. I'm generally asleep or out. Maybe Viola came to see her, I don't know who she saw; it was her time and she had to fill it."

"Did you trust her up there with all the soul brothers?" Coffin Ed asked curiously. "Smalls almost just around the corner and sharp cats cruising up the Avenue all day long in their Cadillacs and Buicks red-hot for a big Southern blonde."

"Hell, if you got to worry about your white chick, you can't afford her," Dick said.

"And you never saw Sugartit before last night?" Grave Digger persisted.

"If you so worried about this mother-raping chick, why don't you go and see her?" Dick asked peevishly.

Coffin Ed looked at his watch. "Three-fourteen," he announced.

"It's too late tonight," Grave Digger said.

Dick looked from one detective to the other, perplexed. "You guys working on this murder case?" he asked.

"Nope, that's homicide, baby," Grave Digger said. "Me and Ed are trying to find out who incited the riot."

Dick's hysterical outburst of laughter seemed odd indeed from so cynical a man.

"Man, that's how you get dandruff," he said.

Interlude

Good people, your food is digested by various juices in the stomach. There is a stomach juice for everything you eat. There is a juice for meat and a juice for potatoes. There is a juice for chitterlings and a juice for sweet potato pie. There is a juice for buttermilk and a juice for hopping John. But sometimes it happens these juices get mixed up and the wrong juice is applied to the wrong food. Now you might eat corn on the cob which has just been taken out of the pot and it's so hot you burn your tongue. Well, your mouth gets mixed up and sends the wrong signal to your stomach. And your stomach hauls off and lets go with the juice for cayenne pepper. Suddenly you got an upset stomach and the hot corn goes to your head. It causes a burning fever and your temperature rises. Your head gets so hot it causes the corn to begin popping. And the popped corn comes through your skull and gets mixed up with your hair. And that's how you get dandruff.

Dusty Fletcher at the Apollo Theater on
125th Street in Harlem

9

A man entered The Temple of Black Jesus. He was a short, fat, black man with a harelip. His face was running with sweat as though his skin was leaking. His short black hair grew so thick on his round inflated head it looked artificial, like drip-dry hair. His body looked blown up like that of a rubber man. The sky-blue silk suit he wore on this hot night glinted with a blue light. He looked inflammable. But he was cool.

Black people milling along the sidewalk stared at him with a mixture of awe and deference. He was the latest.

"Ham, baby," someone whispered.

"Naw, dass Jesus baby," was the harsh rejoinder.

The black man walked forward down a urine-stinking hallway beneath the feet of a gigantic black plaster of paris image of Jesus Christ, hanging by his neck from the rotting white ceiling of a large square room. There was an expression of teeth-bared rage on Christ's black face. His arms were spread, his fists balled, his toes curled. Black blood dripped from red nail holes. The legend underneath read:

THEY LYNCHED ME.

Soul brothers believed it.

The Temple of Black Jesus was on 116th Street, west of Lenox Avenue. It and all the hot dirty slum streets running parallel into Spanish Harlem were teeming with hot dirty slum-dwellers, like cockroaches eating from a bowl of frijoles. Dirt rose from their shuffling feet. Fried hair melted in the hot dark air and ran like grease down sweating black necks. Half-naked people cursed, muttered, shouted, laughed, drank strong whiskey, ate greasy food, breathed rotten air, sweated, stank and celebrated.

This was *The Valley*. Gethsemane was a hill. It was cooler. These people celebrated hard. The heat scrambled their brains, came out their skulls, made dandruff. Normal life was so dark with fear and misery, a celebration went off like a skyrocket. *Nat Turner* day! Who knew who Nat Turner was? Some thought he was a jazz musician teaching the angels jazz; others thought he was a prizefighter teaching the devil to fight. Most agreed the best thing he ever did was die and give them a holiday.

A chickenshit pimp was pushing his two-dollar whore into a dilapidated convertible to drive her down to Central Park to work. Her black face was caked with white powder, her mascaraed eyes dull with stupidity, her thick lips shining like a red fire engine. Time to catch whitey as he slunk around the Lagoon looking to change his luck.

Eleven black nuns came out of a crumbling, dilapidated private house which had a sign in the window reading: FUNERALS PERFORMED. They were carrying a brass four-poster bed as though it were a coffin. The bed had a mattress. On the mattress was a nappy, unkempt head of an old man, sticking from beneath a dirty sheet. He lay so still he might have been dead. No one asked.

In the Silver Moon greasy-spoon restaurant a whiskey-happy joker yelled at the short-order cook behind the counter, "Gimme a cup of coffee as strong as Muhammed Ali and a Mittenburger."

"What kind of burger is that?" the cook asked, grinning.

"Baby, that's burger mit kraut."

To one side of the entrance to the movie theater an old man had a portable barbecue pit made out of a perforated washtub attached to the chassis of a baby carriage. The grill was covered with sizzling pork ribs. The scent of scorching meat rose from the greasy smoke, filled the hot thick air, made mouths water. Half-naked black people crowded about, buying red-hot slabs on pale white bread, crunching the half-cooked bones.

Another old man, clad in his undershirt, had crawled onto the marquee of the movie, equipped with a fishing pole, line, sinker and hook and was fishing for ribs as though they were fish. When the barbecue man's head was turned he would hook a slab of barbecue and haul it up out of sight. Everyone except the barbecue man saw what was happening, but no one gave him away. They grinned at one another, but when the barbecue man looked their way, the grins disappeared.

The barbecue man felt something was wrong. He became suspicious. Then he noticed some of his ribs were missing. He reached underneath his pit and took out a long iron poker.

"What one of you mother-rapers stole my ribs?" he asked, looking mean and dangerous.

No one replied.

"If I catch a mother-raper stealing my ribs, I'll knock out his brains," he threatened.

They were happy people. They liked a good joke. They believed in a Prophet named Ham. They welcomed the Black Jesus to their neighborhood. The white Jesus hadn't done anything for them.

When Prophet Ham entered the chapel, he found it filled with black preachers as he'd expected. Faces gleamed with sweat in the sweltering heat like black painted masks. The air was thick with the odors of bad breath, body sweat and deodorants. But no one smoked.

Prophet Ham took the empty seat on the rostrum and looked at the sea of black faces. His own face assumed as benign an expression as the harelip would permit. An expectant hush fell over the assemblage. The speaker, a portly black man in a black suit, turned off his harangue like a tap and bowed toward Prophet Ham obsequiously.

"And now our Prophet has arrived," he said with his eyes popping expressively. "Our latterday Moses, who shall lead us out of the wilderness. I give you Prophet Ham."

The assembled preachers allowed themselves a lapse of dignity and shouted and amened like paid shills at a revival meeting. Prophet Ham received this acclaim with a frown of displeasure. He stepped to the dais and glared at his audience. He looked indignant.

"Don't call me a Prophet," he said. He had a sort of rumbling lisp and a tendency to slobber when angry. He was angry now. "Do you know what a Prophet is? A Prophet is a misfit that has visions. All the Prophets in history were either epileptics, syphilitics, schizophrenics, sadists or just plain monsters. I just got this harelip. That doesn't make me eligible."

His red eyes glowed, his silk suit glinted, his black face glistened, his split red gums bared from his big yellow teeth.

No one disputed him.

"Neither am I a latterday Moses," he went on. "First of all, Moses was white. I'm black. Second, Moses didn't lead his people out the wilderness until they revolted. First he led them into the wilderness to starve and eat roots. Moses was a square. Instead of leading his people out of Egypt he should have taken over Egypt, then their problems would have been solved."

"But you're a race leader," a preacher shouted from the audience.

"I ain't a race leader neither," he denied. "Does I look like I can race? That's the trouble with you so-called Negroes. You're always looking for a race leader. The only place to race whitey is on the cinder track. We beats him there all right, but that's all. And it ain't you and me who's racing, it's our children. And what are we doing to reward them for winning? Talking all this foolishness about Prophets and race leaders."

"Well, if you ain't a Prophet and ain't a race leader, what is you?" the preacher said.

"I'm a soldier," Prophet Ham said. "I'm a plain and simple soldier in this fight for right. Just call me General Ham. I'm your commander. We got to fight, not race."

Now they had got that point settled, his audience could relax. He wasn't a prophet, and he wasn't a race leader, but they were just as satisfied with him being a general.

"General Ham, baby," a young preacher cried enthusiastically, expressing the sentiment of all. "You command, we obey."

"First we're gonna draft Jesus." He held up his hand to forestall comment. "I know what you're gonna say. You're gonna say other black men, more famous and with a bigger following than me, are employing the Jesus pitch. You're gonna say it's been the custom and habit of our folks for years past to call on Jesus for everything, food, health, justice, mercy, or what have you. But there're two differences. They been calling on the white Jesus. And mostly they been praying for mercy. You know that's the truth.

You are all men of the cloth. All black preachers. All guilty of the same sin. Asking the white Jesus for mercy. For to solve your problem. For to take your part against the white man. And all he tell you is to turn the other cheek. You think he gonna tell you to slap back? He's white too. Whitey is his brother. In fact whitey made him. You think he gonna take your part against his own creator? What kind of thinking is that?"

The preachers laughed with embarrassment. But they heard him.

"We hear you, General Ham, baby. . . . You right, baby. . . . We been praying to the wrong Jesus. . . . Now we pray to the Black Jesus."

"Just like you so-called Negroes," General Ham lisped scornfully. "Always praying. Believing in the philosophy of forgiveness and love. Trying to overcome by love. That's the white Jesus's philosophy. It won't work for you. It only work for whitey. It's whitey's con. Whitey invented it, just like he invented the white Jesus. We're gonna drop the praying altogether."

A shocked silence followed this pronouncement. After all they were preachers. They'd been praying even before they started preaching. They didn't know what to say.

But the young preacher spoke out again. He was young enough to try anything. The old-fashioned praying hadn't done much good. "You command us, General," he said again. He wasn't afraid of change. "We'll give up the praying. Then what'll we do?"

"We ain't gonna ask the Black Jesus for no mercy," General Ham declared. "We ain't gonna ask him for nothing. We just gonna take him and feed him to whitey in the place of the other food we been putting on whitey's table since the first of us arrived as slaves. We been feeding whitey all these years. You know that's the truth. He grown fat and prosperous on the food we been feeding him. Now we're gonna feed him the flesh of the Black Jesus. I don't have to tell you the flesh of Jesus is indigestible. They ain't even digested the flesh of the white Jesus in these two thousand years. And they been eating him every Sunday. Now the flesh of the Black Jesus is even more indigestible. Everybody knows that black meat is harder to digest than white meat. And that, brothers, *IS OUR SECRET WEAPON!*" he shouted with a spray of spit. "That is how we're going to fight whitey and beat him at last. We're gonna keep feeding him the flesh of the Black Jesus until he perish of constipation if he don't choke to death first."

The elderly black preachers were scandalized.

"You don't mean the sacrament?" one asked.

"Is we gonna manufacture wafers?" another asked.

"We'll do it, but how?" the young preacher asked sensibly.

"We're gonna march with the statue of the Black Jesus until whitey pukes," General Ham said.

With the image of the lynched Jesus which hung in the entrance in their minds, the preachers saw what he meant.

"What you need for the march, General?" asked the young black preacher, who was practical.

General Ham appreciated this practicality. "Marchers," he replied. "Nothing takes the place of marchers for a march," he said, "but money. So if we can't find the marchers we get some money and buy them. I'm gonna make you my second in command, young man. What is your name?"

"I'm Reverend Duke, General."

"From now on you're a Colonel, Reverend Duke. I call you Colonel Duke. I want you to get these marchers lined up in front of this temple by ten o'clock."

"That don't give us much time, General. Folks is celebrating."

"Then make it a celebration, Colonel," General Ham said. "Get some banners reading 'Jesus baby'. Give us a little sweet wine. Sing 'Jesus Savior'. Get some of these gals from the streets. Tell 'em you want 'em for the dance. They ask what dance? You tell 'em *the* dance. Wherever gals go, mens follow. Remember that, Colonel. That's the first principle of the march. You dig me, Colonel?"

"We dig you, General," said Colonel Duke.

"Then I see you-all at the march," General Ham said and left.

Outside on 116th Street, a lavender Cadillac Coupe de Ville convertible, trimmed in yellow metal which the black people passing thought was gold, was parked at the curb. A buxom white woman with blue-dyed gray hair, green eyes and a broad flat nose, wearing a décolleté dress in orange chiffon, sat behind the wheel. Huge rose breasts popped from the orange dress as though expanded by the heat, and rested on the steering-wheel. When General Ham approached and opened the door on his side, she looked around and gave him a smile that lit up the night. Her two upper incisors were crowned with shining gold with a diamond between. "Daddy," she greeted. "What took you so long?"

"I been cooking with Jesus," he lisped, settling into the seat beside her.

She chuckled. It was a fat woman's chuckle. It sounded like hot fat bubbling. She pulled out in front of a bus and drove down the crowded street as though black people were invisible. They got the hell out of her way.

10

Sergeant Ryan came up from the cellar to take over the questioning. He brought along his photographer, Ted, who had finished taking pictures, to get him out of the way of the fingerprint crew who were still at work.

The rooms were small. Each was equipped with a built-in washbasin and clothes closet and a radiator, and furnished with a double bed and dressing-table of oak veneer. All the shades were drawn on the windows on the other side, and the rooms were hot and airless as though sealed. All were alike with the exception of the front room which had a second window on the street, from which the tenant could have stolen the hats from the heads of passersby to go along with all his suits and shirts. With the addition of four detectives they were crowded.

A couple by the name of Mr and Mrs Tola Onan Ramsey occupied the front room. Tola was a presser at a downtown cleaners and his wife, Bee, ironed shirts at the laundry next door. Tola said the suits and shirts were his own which he had bought and paid for with his own money, and he didn't need any hats. The local detectives kept quiet, but they wondered why the Ramseys paid the extra rent for the front room when any of the back rooms would have served them just as well. All they were doing was stealing from their bosses and the extra front window was an unnecessary expense. Bee called Coffin Ed aside to ask him if he wanted to buy some shirts cheap, while Tola was denying to Sergeant Ryan seeing anything, hearing anything or knowing anything. He and Bee had been in bed sound asleep, as hard as they had worked all day, and they hadn't even heard the neighbors in the hall or the people on the sidewalk who, as a rule, sounded as though they were passing through their room.

Sergeant Ryan soon gave up on them. They were too innocent for him. They were the most law-abiding, hardworking, know-nothing colored people he had ever seen. Neither Grave Digger nor Coffin Ed batted an eye.

The couple in the middle room called themselves Mr and Mrs Socrates X. Hoover. He was a tall, lanky black man with buck teeth and dusty-colored burred hair. His stringy muscles jerked like dying snakes beneath his sweating black skin and his small red eyes glowed with agitation under the scrutiny of the detectives. He sat on the edge of the bed clad only in the dirty jeans he'd slipped on hurriedly to open the door for the law, while his woman lay naked beneath the sheet, which she had drawn up to her mouth. She was a big yellow woman with red hair, straightened by a pressing-iron, sticking out from her head in all directions.

He said there was no need of them sniffing so mother-raping suspiciously, that smell came from the cubebs he smoked for his asthma. And she had been straightening her hair, she added, as they could oughta tell from the iron on the dresser. When Grave Digger continued to look skeptical, she flew salty and said if they smelt where she'd been making love with her own husband, that was only natural. What kind of minds did they have? Far as she knew, only white folks knew how to make love without its smelling.

Sergeant Ryan turned bright red.

Socrates said he made an honest living parking cars at the Yankee Stadium. Last winter? He hadn't been here last winter. Sergeant Ryan dropped it and asked what she did. She said she kept appointments. What kind of appointments? Do they have to be some special kind? Just appointments, that's all. Sergeant Ryan tried to catch the eye of one of the colored detectives, but they refused to be caught.

About what had gone on outside their room that night, or any other night, they knew less than their neighbors at the front. They always kept their shades drawn and their window closed to keep out the noise and the smells and they couldn't hear anything inside, not even their neighbors. Sergeant Ryan was silent for a moment while they all listened to the sound of a drawer being opened and the exchange of voices in the adjoining room, but he didn't pursue it. What about when one of them went to the toilet? he asked instead. Poon became so agitated she sat up in bed, exposing two big drooping breasts encircled by deed red marks where her brassière had cut her and tipped by tough brown teats like the stalks of pumpkins cut from the vine. Go to the crapper? What for? They weren't children, they didn't pee in bed. Grave Digger glanced at the washbasin with such obvious suggestion her face swelled with indignation and the sheet flew from the rest of her, revealing her big hairy nest. Suddenly the room was flooded with the strong alkaloid scent of continuous sexual intercourse. Sergeant Ryan threw up his hands.

When things had calmed down he listened to them deny any knowledge of the cellar at all. They might have noticed the door at the side, but neither remembered. If they were directly over the cellar and boiler room, they had never heard any sounds from down there. They weren't living there in the winter. They didn't know who had lived there before them. They never saw anybody going or coming from around the side. No, they had never seen any strange white men in the whole neighborhood. Nor strange white women either.

By the time the sergeant got to the tenants in the last room he was well browned off. These people called themselves Mr and

Mrs Booker T. Washington. Booker said he was the manager of a recreation hall on upper Seventh Avenue. What kind of recreation? Recreation, where people play. Play what? Play pool. So you're a hustler around the pool hall? I'm the manager. What's the name of it? Acey-Deucey's? What's that? Onesy-twosy's. Oh, you said ace and deuce's. Nawsuh, I said Acey-Deucey's. All right, all right, and what's your wife's name? Madame Booker, she answered for herself. She was another big-titted yellow woman with straightened red hair. And he was lean, black and red-eyed like his neighbor. The sergeant wondered what it was about these lean, hungry-looking red-eyed black men that these big yellow women liked so well. And what did Madame Booker do for her living? She didn't have to do nothing but look after her husband but she told fortunes ever now and then just to pass away the time 'cause her husband worked at nights. The sergeant looked at the television set on the deal table and the transistor radio on the end of the dressing-table next to the bed. But he let it go. Who were her customers — clients? People. What kind of people? Just people is all. Men? Women? Men and women. Did she have any white men among her clients? No, she never told white men's fortunes. Why, were the augurs bad in Harlem? She didn't know whether the augurs were bad or good, just none had ever asked her.

Further questioning elicited the facts that they had seen, heard, and knew even less than both their neighbors put together. They didn't have anything to do with the other people who lived in that house, not that they were hincty, but there were some bad people who lived there. Who? They didn't know exactly. Well, where, then? On this floor? The second floor? The third floor? They couldn't say exactly, sommers in the building. Well, how did they know they were bad if they didn't know them? They could tell by looking at them. Sergeant Ryan reminded them that they had just claimed they never saw anyone. What they meant was going sommers; 'course they saw people in the hall but they didn't know where they were going or where they had been. And they never saw any white men in the hall going somewhere or coming from somewhere? Never, only once a month the man came around for the rent. Well, what was his name? the sergeant asked quickly, thinking he was getting somewhere. They didn't know. Did they mean to tell him they paid a man the rent whom they didn't know? They meant they didn't know his name but they knew he was the man, all right; he was the same man who had been there ever since they had been there. And how long had they been there? They had been there going on for three years. Then they had been there during the winter? Two winters. Then they knew about the cellar? Knew what about the cellar? That there was one? Their eyes popped. 'Course there was a cellar, how else could the superintendent fire the boiler if there wasn't no cellar? It was a question, the sergeant admitted. And who was the superintendent? A West Indian named Lucas Covey. Is he colored? Colored? Whoever heard of a white West Indian? The sergeant admitted they had him there. And did this, er, Mr Covey live in the cellar? Live in the cellar! How could he? There wasn't no place for him to live there, les' it was 'side the boiler. What about the empty room? Empty room! What empty room? Well, then when was the last time they had been in the cellar? They hadn't never been in the cellar, they just knew there had to be one to hold the boiler 'cause they had central heating, and it came from somewhere.

The sergeant took out his handkerchief to wipe the sweat from his face, but remembered he had used it to open the bloodstained door in the cellar and put it back into his pocket, wiping his forehead with his coat sleeve instead.

Well, then, where did Mr Covey live if he didn't live in the cellar? he asked desperately. He lived in his other house on 122nd Street. What was the number? They didn't know the number, but it was a brick house just like this one only it was twice as wide and it was the second house from the corner of Eighth Avenue. He couldn't miss it, the name was over the door. It was called *Cozy Flats*.

The sergeant figured he'd had enough of that. He saw no reason to take any of them in as yet. The next thing was to find Lucas Covey. But when they got out in the hall the photographer discovered his pocket camera was missing. So they started over with the Washingtons. But they hadn't seen his camera. Then they went back to the Hoovers.

"Bless my soul, I wondered where this Kodak came from," Poon said. "I was reaching for a cigarette and found it lying there on the floor."

The red-faced photographer took his camera and put it back into his pocket and opened his mouth to state his mind, but Grave Digger cut him off.

"That could get you ninety days," he told Socrates.

"For what? I ain't done nothing."

"Oh, hell, skip it," the sergeant said. "Let's get out of here."

They stopped on the street to wait for the fingerprint crew who were just coming up from the cellar, and he asked the colored detectives, "Do you believe any of that horse manure?"

"Hell, it ain't a question of believing it. We found them all at home, in bed, asleep for all we know. How do we know they heard, saw or know anything? All we can do is take their word."

"I mean that shit about their occupations."

"If you're worried about that you may as well go home," Coffin Ed said.

"Well, it's half-true, like everything else," Grave Digger said pacifyingly. "We know Booker T. Washington hangs around Acey-Deucey's poolroom where he earns a little scratch racking balls when he hasn't snatched a purse that paid. And we know that Socrates Hoover watches parked cars at night on the side streets around Yankee Stadium to keep them from being robbed of anything he can rob himself. And what else can two big yellow whores do but hustle? That's why those sports make themselves scarce at night. But Tola Ramsey and his wife do just what they say. It's easy enough to check. But all you got to do is look at all those suits and shirts which don't fit him."

"Anyway, none of them work in white folks' kitchens," Coffin Ed said gruffly.

Faces turned red all over the place.

"Why would anyone live here who was honest?" Grave Digger said. "Or how could anyone stay honest who lived here? What do you want? This place was built for vice, for whores to hustle in and thieves to hide out in. And somebody got a building permit, because it's been built after the ghetto got here." He paused for a moment. They were all silent. "Anything else?" he asked.

The sergeant let the subject drop. He ordered the fingerprint crew to stick around and they followed his car in their car while Coffin Ed and Grave Digger brought up the rear. The three cars of detectives descended on 122nd Street like the rat exterminators, but not a soul was in sight, not even a rat. Coffin Ed checked with his watch. It was 3:37. He buzzed Lieutenant Anderson at the precinct station.

"It's me and Digger, boss. You find any fez-headed men?"

"Plenty of them. Seventeen to be precise. But none with extra pants. You still with Ryan?"

"Right behind him."

"Find out anything?"

"Nothing that can't keep."

"All right, stick with him."

When he had rung off, Grave Digger said, "What did he think we were going to do, go fishing?"

Coffin Ed grunted.

Take two crumbling, neglected, overcrowded brick buildings like the one they had just left, slam them together with a hallway down the middle like a foul-air sandwich, put two cement columns flanking a dirt-darkened glass-panelled door, and put the words, COZY FLATS, on the transom, and you have an incubator of depravity. There one could find all the vices of Harlem in microcosm: sex perversions, lesbians, pederasts, pot smokers, riders of the LSD, street hustlers and their cretinistic pimps sleeping in the same beds where they turned their tricks, daisy chains, sex circuses, and caterers to the society trade: wife-swappers, gang-fuckers, seekers of depravity – name it, they had it.

But all the detectives found were closed doors, bedroom and toilet odors, the nose pinching smell of marijuana, the grunting and groaning of skin poppers and homosexuals, the muted whine of old blues played low.

The graffiti on the walls of the ground-floor hall gave the illusion of primitive painting of pygmies affected with elephantiasis of the genitals. A sign over a small green door beneath the staircase read: SUPERINTENDENT.

Sniffing the smells suggested by the graffiti, the sergeant said cynically, "Sin made easy."

"You call this easy?" Grave Digger flared. "You mean *hot*!"

Five minutes of hammering brought the superintendent up the stairs to open his door. He gave the appearance of having been asleep. He was clad in an old blue flannel robe with a frayed belt worn over wrinkled cotton pajamas with wide violently clashing red and blue stripes. His short kinky hair was burred from contact with the pillow and his smooth black skin had a tracery of lines as though the witches had been riding him. He held a blued steel .45 Colt automatic in his right hand and it was pointed on the level of their stomachs. He raked them with furious red eyes.

"What you want?"

The sergeant hastened with his shield. "We're the police."

"So what! You woke me out of a dead sleep."

"All right," Grave Digger said roughly. "You've made your point."

Slowly the man returned the automatic to the pocket of his robe, still holding it.

"You're Mr Covey, the superintendent?" the sergeant verified.

"Yeah, that's me."

"You always answer your door with a pistol?"

"You never know who's knocking at this time o' morning."

"Back up, buster, and let us in," Grave Digger said.

"You're the law," the man acknowledged, turning to precede them down the flight of brick stairs.

Grave Digger's first impression was he looked too arrogant to be the super of a joint like this, unless he had all the tenants working for him, like a sort of black Fagin. In which case, his being black would account for his arrogance.

To the average eye he was a thin superior-acting black man with a long smooth narrow face and a cranium that was almost a perfect ellipsoid. His thick-lipped mouth was as wide as his face and when he talked his lips curled back from even white teeth. His eyes had a slight Mongolian slant, giving his face a bitsa look, a bit of African, a bit of Nordic, a bit of Oriental. He was proud and handsome but there was a bit of effeminacy in his carriage. He looked very sure of himself.

The only thing missing was the sleep in the corners of his eyes.

Flinging open the door of his bedroom, he said, "*Entrez.*"

The bedroom held a three-quarter bed that had been slept in; a rolltop desk with a green blotter, telephone, and desk chair; night-table with ashtray; television set on its separate stand and overstuffed leather armchair facing it, dressing table with black and white dolls flanking the mirror. Beyond the boiler room was a room used for a kitchen-dining-room and a shower room off from it with a toilet.

"You're fixed up cozy enough," Sergeant Ryan said. He had brought a fingerprint man and his photographer with him, and they grinned dutifully.

"That bother you?" Covey challenged.

The sergeant dropped all pleasantries, and began asking questions. Covey said he had been to the Apollo Theater and seen a gangster film called *Double or Nothing* and a stage show which had The Supremes and Martha and The Vandellas and television comedian Bill Cosby, along with the house orchestra. Afterwards he had stopped at the bar of Frank's Restaurant and had a bean and cornbeef sandwich and had walked home down Eighth Avenue.

"You can check that?" Ryan said to the precinct detectives.

"Not easily," Grave Digger admitted. "Everybody goes to the Apollo and Frank's bar is so crowded at that time of night only celebrities stand out."

Covey hadn't seen anyone on entering the apartment and he lived alone so that once he was down in his hole he didn't see anyone until he came up the next day. If it wasn't for the garbage stinking if he didn't put it out, he could be down here dead for weeks and no one would notice. Didn't he have other duties besides putting out the garbage? In the winter he fired the boilers. Didn't he have any relatives? Sure, plenty, but they were all in Jamaica and he hadn't seen any of them since he had come to New York three years previous. Friends? Money was a man's only friend. Women? "What a question," Coffin Ed muttered, looking at the dolls. The sergeant reddened. Covey got on his dignity. There were women everywhere, he said. "Damn right," Grave Digger said. The sergeant dropped it. Who cleaned up, then? The tenants cleaned in front of their doors and the wind blew the dirt off the street. Well, all right, did he know about the cellar in the other house? Cellar? Basement? What about the basement? About the furnished room? Naturally he knew about the furnished room, he was the superintendent, wasn't he? Well, then, who did he rent it to? Rent it to? He didn't rent it to nobody. Who lived in it, then? Didn't nobody live in it in the summer; the company built it for a helper to sleep in in the winter — someone to fire the boiler. What company was that? The owners, Acme Realty; they owned lots of buildings in Harlem. Was he the superintendent for them all? No, just these two. Did he know the officials of the company? No, just the building manager and the rent collector. Well, where were they located? They had an office on lower Broadway, in the Knickerbocker Building, just south of Canal Street. And what were the names of the men he knew? Well, Mr Shelton was the building manager and Lester Chambers was the rent collector. West Indians too? No, they were white. The sergeant dropped it. Well, to get back to the room in the other basement, could anyone live there without his knowing it? Not hardly, he was over there every morning to put out the garbage. But it was possible? Everything was possible, but it wasn't likely anybody would be living there with him not knowing; 'cause first they'd have to get in and the outside door had a Yale lock and he had the only two keys. He went across the room and took a large ring of keys from a hook on the wall beside the door and exhibited two brass Yale keys. And if they was to break in, he would see it first thing he got there to put out the garbage. But they could have had a key made? the sergeant persisted. Covey ran a hand over his burrs. What was he trying to get at? The sergeant asked his own question in reply. He had looked into the basement recently? Covey looked around impatiently; his gaze met Coffin Ed's; he looked away. What for? he countered. The place was only used in the winter; it was kept closed and locked in the summer to keep young punks from taking girls down there to rape them. He was a mighty distrustful man, the sergeant observed. Meeting people at the door with a pistol in his hand, thinking of teen-agers as rapists. The colored detectives joined Covey in a condescending smile. The sergeant noticed it, but passed it by. Did he, Covey, know what kind of people lived in these buildings he served? Naturally, he was the superintendent; all respectable, hard-working, honest, married people, like all Harlem tenants of Acme Realty. The sergeant's face was a picture of incredulity; he didn't know whether Covey was making fun of him or not. Coffin Ed and Grave Digger kept their faces absolutely blank. Well, someone had been living in the furnished room of that other basement, the sergeant announced abruptly. Impossible! Covey denied promptly. If anyone had been down there all the tenants on the ground floor would know about it for you could hear through that floor as good as you could hear through those walls. Then somebody was lying, the sergeant said, because not only had someone been living there but a man had been killed there only a few hours ago. Covey's eyes widened slowly until all the other features looked disarranged in his narrow face.

"You kidding, aren't you?" His voice was a shocked whisper.

"I'm not kidding," the sergeant said. "His throat was cut."

"I was just by there yesdiddy morning."

"You're going back this morning. Now! Put your clothes on. And give me that gun."

Covey moved in a daze, handing over the pistol docilely as he might have passed a plate. He looked stunned. "It ain't possible," he kept muttering to himself.

But sight of the bloody furnished room changed that quickly to rage. "Them mother-rapers upstairs know about it," he raved. "You couldn't cut a man down here without them hearing him scream."

They took him upstairs and confronted him with each of the three couples. Other than the vilest language that he had ever heard, the sergeant learned nothing new. Covey couldn't shake the tenants' story that they hadn't heard anything, and they couldn't shake his that he hadn't known about the room.

"Let's make an experiment," the sergeant said. "Ted, you and this man — what's your name? Stan. You and Stan go down in the basement and yell, and the rest of us will stand in each of the rooms up here and see if we can hear you."

Putting their ears to the floor they could hear faintly in the middle room, occupied by Socrates and Poon Hoover, but they doubted if they could hear lying in the bed, although they didn't try. But they couldn't hear in the front and back rooms, nor in the kitchen which they tried too. But they could hear quite clearly in the hall and strangely enough they could hear in the john.

"Well, that narrows it down to everybody who was awake in the whole of Harlem," the sergeant said disgustedly. "You people go back to bed."

"What you want us to do with this one?" the white detectives who were flanking Covey asked.

"Hell, we'll take him on back and call it a day. None of these people can get anywhere, and maybe by tomorrow my brains won't be so fuzzy."

When Covey had disappeared through the entrance of the Cozy Flats, Coffin Ed got out of the car beside Grave Digger, and called, "Hey, wait a minute; I left my sound meter in your flat." But Covey didn't hear him.

"Go and get it," Grave Digger said. "I'll wait for you."

The white detectives looked at each other curiously. They hadn't seen Coffin Ed's sound meter either. But it wasn't anything to work up a sweat about; they all wanted to get home. But the sergeant wanted to have a word with the colored precinct detectives before he turned in so the fingerprint crew drove off and left him with his two disgruntled assistants, the photographer, Ted, and his driver, Joe.

Coffin Ed had been slightly surprised to find Covey's hall door unlocked, but he didn't hesitate. He went down silently and opened the door of Covey's bed-sitting-room without knocking and went inside.

Covey was leaning back in his desk chair with a wide, taunting grin. "I knew you'd follow me, you old fox. You thought you'd catch me telephoning. But I don't know nothing 'bout this business. I'm as clean as a minister's dick."

"That's too mother-raping bad," Coffin Ed said, his burn-scarred face twitching like a French version of *the jerk*, as he moved in with his long nickel-plated, head-whipping pistol swinging in his hand. "Your ass pays for it."

Grave Digger didn't want to talk to the sergeant at that moment, so he radio-phoned Lieutenant Anderson at the precinct station.

"It's me, Digger."

"What's new?"

"Count me ninety seconds."

Without another word, Anderson began, "One, two, three. . . ." Not too fast, not too slow. At " . . . ninety . . . ", Grave Digger slid across the seat and got out on the sidewalk and went towards the entrance of the Cozy Flats, loosening his pistol as he went.

"Hey . . . " the sergeant called, but he made as though he didn't hear him and went through the entrance and down the front hall.

When he entered Covey's bedroom, he found him lying sideways across the bed, a red bruise aslant his forehead, his left eye shut and bleeding, his upper lip swollen to the size of a bicycle tire, and Coffin Ed atop him with a knee in his solar plexus, choking him to death.

He clutched Coffin Ed by the back of the collar and pulled him back. "Leave him able to talk."

Coffin Ed looked down at the swollen bloody face beneath him. "You want to talk, don't you, mother?"

"Rented to a business man — salesman — nice man —" Covey gasped. "Nice — wanted place to rest — afternoons — John Babson — nice man. . . . "

"White man?"

"Seal brown. Brown-colored man. . . . "

"What's his pet name?"

"Pet name — pet name —"

"His loving name, mother-raper?"

"I — tole you — all . . . I know. . . . "

Coffin Ed drew back his right fist as though he would hit him and his left hand flew to his mouth. Hitting at him from beyond, from where he was standing at the head of the bed, with the long heavy barrel of his pistol, Grave Digger struck with such force he knocked the back of his hand into his mouth so hard that when he pulled it away screaming, three of the front teeth that Coffin Ed had loosened previously, were embedded in the carpal bones of his hand. "*Jesus Baby*!" he gasped.

The sergeant burst through the door, followed by his wide-eyed assistants. "What the hell" he exclaimed.

"Fascists!" Covey screamed when he saw the white men. "Racists! Black brutes!"

"Take this mother-raper before we kill him," Grave Digger said.

11

Captain Brice was waiting for them when they came up from questioning Dick. He sat in his own chair, leaning back with his polished black oxfords atop the desk. With his thick torso encased in a dark blue Brooks Brothers mohair suit, along with his carefully parted hair and knotted blue silk tie, he looked for all the world like a midtown banker just returned from the annual stag party. Anderson sat submissively in the visitor's chair across the desk from him.

"How was the champagne, sir?" Grave Digger needled.

"Not bad, not bad," Captain Brice replied, not to be outdone. But everyone knew he hadn't come to the district at three o'clock in the morning just to pass the time of day.

"Lieutenant Anderson tells me you've been interrogating the two star witnesses in that family slaughter on Sugar Hill," he went on, taking a serious tone.

"Yes, sir, it was a rejuvenation pitch, but you probably know more about it than we do," Grave Digger said.

"Well, there's nothing new about it. Did you find out where the pitch originated?"

"Yes, sir, it originated with Christ," Grave Digger said with a straight face. "But there are a couple of things about this particular shindig up there that need answering."

"Let homicide answer them," Captain Brice said. "You're precinct men."

"Maybe they ought to state it," Anderson interjected.

"There's been too much of that now, interfering in homicide's business," Captain Brice said. "It's given our precinct a bad rep."

"I booked them as material witnesses and we're holding them here until the magistrate's court sets bail," Anderson said, standing up for his men. "I had them question the witnesses."

Captain Brice decided he didn't want a run-in with his lieutenant. "All right," he conceded, turning back to Grave Digger. "What needs answering that homicide doesn't know?"

"We don't know what homicide know," Grave Digger admitted. "But we'd like to know what's become of the money."

Captain Brice took his feet from the desk and sat up. "What money?"

Grave Digger reported what his witnesses had said about a Gladstone bag filled with money.

Captain Brice leaned forward and stared dogmatically, "You can forget about the money. Sam didn't have any money unless he stole it, and if that's the case it'll come out."

"Did either of the witnesses actually see the money?" Anderson persisted.

"No, but both of them believed for other reasons — which I will tell you if you want to hear them—" Anderson shook his head — "that the bag was filled with money," Grave Digger continued.

"You can forget the money," Captain Brice repeated. "Do you think I could have been Captain for this precinct as long as I have and not know who owns what in my bailiwick?"

"Then what's happened to the Gladstone bag?"

"If there was one. You only have the word of two witnesses and they were involved — one his son and the other his daughter-in-law; and now they're the heirs of his estate if it is found that he had any estate."

"If there was a Gladstone bag, it'll turn up," Anderson said.

Captain Brice took a fat cigar from a leather case in his inside pocket. No one offered him a light. They watched him bite off the end and roll the cigar between his lips. They let him search through his pockets until he found a book of paper matches and they watched him light the end of his cigar. Anderson took out his pipe and filled it with the same deliberation but Coffin Ed stepped forward and held a lighted match for him. Captain Brice reddened, but otherwise acted as though he hadn't noticed. Grave Digger gave his partner a reproachful look. Anderson hid behind a cloud of smoke.

"What's the other question?" Captain Brice asked coldly.

"Who killed Doctor Mubuta?"

"Goddammit, the chauffeur killed him. Don't try to make a mystery out of this nigger mess."

"Johnson X couldn't have killed him," Coffin Ed contradicted, more from the pleasure of contradicting the Captain than from any reasoned conclusion.

"Homicide is satisfied with him," Captain Brice stated, trying to avoid an argument with the two colored detectives.

"They'd be satisfied hanging the rap on anybody called X," Coffin Ed went on.

"Anyway, it's too early to tell," Grave Digger entered a conciliatory tone. "I suppose homicide is having the fluid analyzed?"

"That's obvious," Anderson said. "I smelt it myself. It's cyanide."

"Not even colored folk's poison," Coffin Ed muttered.

"It served its purpose," Captain Brice said harshly. "Sam was a pain in the ass."

"Fronting for the Syndicate? Why'd you let him? It's your bailiwick, as you just said," Grave Digger questioned.

"He had a licensed loan and mortgage business. He had a legal right to operate as many so-called offices as he wished. There was nothing I could do."

"Well, Doctor Mubuta has solved that; now you only got the Syndicate to deal with," Grave Digger observed.

Captain Brice banged his fist so hard on his desk top the cigar flew from his fingers and landed on the floor at Coffin Ed's feet. "Goddamn the Syndicate! I'll have the numbers out of Harlem before a week's gone by."

Grave Digger looked skeptical.

Coffin Ed picked up the Captain's cigar and returned it to him with such elaborate politeness he seemed to be poking fun. The Captain threw his cigar into the spittoon without looking at it. Anderson peered around his smoke screen to see if the land was safe.

"What you want us to do at night?" Grave Digger asked pointedly, reminding him that the numbers for the most part were a daytime racket.

"I want you two men to keep on this riot bit that the lieutenant assigned you to," he said. "You're my two best men and I want you to clean up this precinct. I feel like the lieutenant that these brush-fire riots are being instigated and I want you to nab the instigator."

"Cleanup campaign, eh?" Coffin Ed sneered.

"It's about time, isn't it?" Anderson said.

Captain Brice looked meditatively at Coffin Ed. "You don't like it?" he challenged.

"It's a job," Coffin Ed said enigmatically.

"Why don't you let us talk to the other witnesses, Captain?" Grave Digger intervened.

"The D.A.'s got a homicide bureau for his own use in collecting evidence on homicides," Captain Brice pointed out patiently. "They're attorneys and detectives and laboratory technicians — the whole shooting lot. What do you think you two precinct detectives can uncover that they can't?"

"That very reason. It's our precinct. We might learn something that wouldn't mean a damn thing to them."

"For instance, who's the instigator of these chickenshit riots."

"Maybe," Grave Digger said.

"Well, I'm not going to have it. I know you two guys. You go off cracking heads and shooting people on just a theory, and when it turns out wrong, which is just as liable as not, the commissioner cracks down and the press gets on my ass. It might not bother you two tough customers, maybe you can take it, but it's a black eye for me. I come up for retirement next year and I don't want to leave here with a cloud over my head and a couple of trigger-happy dicks subject to shoot anybody anytime. I want to leave a clean precinct when I leave and a disciplined staff willing to take orders and not try to run the goddamn precinct themselves."

"You mean you want us to lay off before we discover something you don't want discovered?" Grave Digger challenged.

"He means he wants you fellows to lay off status quo before you get all of us into trouble, and yourselves too," Anderson said.

Grave Digger gave him a you-too look.

Captain Brice said, "I mean for you to work on the assignment the lieutenant gave you, and let people better prepared for it handle the homicides. Your assignment is a damn tougher assignment, if you just have to satisfy your yen for being tough, and before you're finished with it you won't feel so darned inclined to make trouble."

"All right, Captain," Grave Digger said. "Don't complain if we come up with the wrong answer."

"I don't want the wrong answer."

"The right answer might be the wrong answer."

Captain Brice glared at Anderson. "And I'm holding you responsible, Lieutenant." Then he turned and looked from one detective to the other. "And if you were white men I'd suspend you for insubordination."

He couldn't have said anything which would have infuriated the black detectives more. They understood at last he meant to muzzle them for the duration. It looked like a two-way play. Anderson, their friend, had given them this impossible assignment; all the Captain had to do was follow it up. Anderson was in line when the Captain bowed out, no doubt with his pockets full of loot. There never was a precinct captain who died broke. And it was to his interests as much as to the Captain's that they didn't rock the boat.

"You don't have no objections to us going and eat?" Grave Digger asked sarcastically. "Plain licensed food?"

The Captain didn't answer.

Anderson glanced at the electric clock on the wall back of the Captain's desk and said, "Check out while you're at it."

They went upstairs to the detectives' room and signed out and went out the back exit past the cop on guard and down the stairs into the brick-walled court where the garage was located. Anderson was waiting for them. The courtyard was brightly lit since Deke O'Malley had escaped that way and Anderson looked frail and strangely vulnerable in the vertical glare.

"I'm sorry," he said. "I saw it coming."

"You sent it," Coffin Ed accused flatly.

"I know what you're thinking, but it won't be for long. Have a little patience. The Captain doesn't want to leave here with the precinct in a turmoil. You can't blame him."

The two black detectives looked at one another. Their short-cropped hair was salted with gray and they were thicker around their middles. Their faces bore the lumps and scars they had collected in the enforcement of law in Harlem. Now after twelve years as first-grade precinct detectives they hadn't been promoted. Their raises in salaries hadn't kept up with the rise of the cost of living. They hadn't finished paying for their houses. Their private cars had been bought on credit. And yet they hadn't taken a dime in bribes. Their entire careers as cops had been one long period of turmoil. When they weren't taking lumps from the thugs, they were taking lumps from the commissioners. Now they were curtailed in their own duties. And they didn't expect it to change.

"We don't blame the Captain," Grave Digger said.

"We're just envious."

"I'll be taking over soon," Anderson sought to console them.

"Damn right," Coffin Ed said, rejecting the sympathy.

Anderson reddened and turned away. "Eat happy," he called over his shoulder, but didn't get a reply.

12

They stood on tiptoe, strained their eyes.

"Let me look."

"Well, look then."

"What you see?"

That was the question. No one saw anything. Then, simultaneously, three distinct groups of marchers came into view.

One came up 125th Street from the east, on the north side of the street, marching west towards the Block. It was led by a vehicle the likes of which many had never seen, and as muddy as though it had come out of East River. A bare-legged black youth hugged the steering-wheel. They could see plainly that he was bare-legged for the vehicle didn't have any door. He, in turn, was being hugged by a bare-legged white youth sitting at his side. It was a brotherly hug, but coming from a white youth it looked suggestive. Whereas the black had looked plain bare-legged, the bare-legged white youth looked stark naked. Such is the way those two colors affect the eyes of the citizens of Harlem. In the South it's just the opposite.

Behind these brotherly youths sat a very handsome young man of sepia color with the strained expression of a man moving his bowels. With him sat a middle-aged white woman in a teen-age dress who looked similarly engaged, with the exception that she had constipation. They held a large banner upright between them which read:

BROTHERHOOD! Brotherly Love Is The Greatest!

Following in the wake of the vehicle were twelve rows of bare-limbed marchers, four in each row, two white and two black, in orderly procession, each row with its own banner identical to the one in the vehicle. Somehow the black youths looked unbelievably black and the white youths unnecessarily white.

These were followed by a laughing, dancing, hugging, kissing horde of blacks and whites of all ages and sexes, most of whom had been strangers to each other a half-hour previous. They looked like a segregationist nightmare. Strangely enough, the black citizens of Harlem were scandalized.

"It's an orgy!" someone cried.

Not to be outdone, another joker shouted, "Mama don't 'low that stuff in here."

A dignified colored lady sniffed. "White trash."

Her equally dignified mate suppressed a grin. "What else, with all them black dustpans?"

But no one showed any animosity. Nor was anyone surprised. It was a holiday. Everyone was ready for anything.

But when attention was diverted to the marchers from the south, many eyes seemed to pop out in black faces. The marchers from the south were coming north on the east side of Seventh Avenue, passing in front of the Scheherazade bar restaurant and the interdenominational church with the coming text posted on the notice-board outside:

SINNERS ARE SUCKERS! DON'T BE A SQUARE!

What caused the eyes of these dazed citizens to goggle was the sight of the apparition out front. Propped erect on the front bumper of a gold-trimmed lavender-colored Cadillac convertible driven by a fat black man with a harelip, dressed in a metallic-blue suit, was the statue of the Black Jesus, dripping black blood from its outstretched hands, a white rope dangling from its broken neck, its teeth bared in a look of such rage and horror as to curdle even blood mixed with as much alcohol as was theirs. Its crossed black feet were nailed to a banner which read: THEY LYNCHED ME! While two men standing in the back of the convertible held aloft another banner reading: BE NOT AFRAID!

In its wake was a long disorganized procession of a startling number of thinly-clad black girls of all shapes and sizes, clinging to the ebony arms of more tee-shirted young men than they had ever been seen outside the army. Teeth shone in black faces, eyes flashed whitely. Some carried banners which read: BLACK JESUS BABY. Others read: CHOKE THEM BABY. They were singing:

"Be not afraid . . . of the dead . . . keep your head, baby, keep your head." They seemed inordinately happy to be following in the wake of such a hideous Jesus. But bringing up the rear was a shuffling mass of solemn preachers with their own banner reading:

FEED THEM JESUS! *They'll vomit every time!*

A devout Christian drunk coming out of the Scheherazade looked up and saw the black apparition being propelled by what looked to him like a burning chariot being driven by the devil in a fireproof suit, and gave a violent start. "I dreamed it," he cried. "That they'd do it again."

But most of the holiday-makers were startled into silence. Caught between a spasm of nausea by the sight of the apparition of the Black Jesus and the contagious happiness of the sea of black youths, their faces twisted in grotesque grimaces for all the world like good Harlem citizens trying out a new French dance.

They were saved from proceeding any further with this new kick by the sound of thunder coming from that section of Seventh Avenue north of the intersection. The marchers from the north were led by two big rugged black men clad in belted leather coats, looking for all the world like Nazi SS troopers in blackface. Behind them marched the two silent clerics who had been seen cooking in Doctor Moore's unfurnished apartment. Behind them came the sweating tallow man who had last been seen atop a barrel at the intersection of 135th Street and Seventh Avenue, raving hysterically about Black Power. Following at a safe distance, two powerful-looking men bared to the waist were pushing a contraption on two wheels greatly resembling the boiler of a locomotive, which rumbled and boomed with the sound of thunder while light flashed from within, lighting up the white crescents of the black men's eyes, the ivory shields of their teeth, and the gleaming black muscles of their naked torsos, like kaleidoscopes of hell. A large white banner, held aloft by two men on their flanks, was also hit by the flashing light, and trembled in the sound of thunder, reading:

BLACK THUNDER! BLACK POWER!

In their wake followed a packed mass of men and women,

dressed in black, who, upon closer inspection, looked of extraordinary size. Their banners read simply: BLACK POWER. In the dim light they looked serious. Their faces looked grave. If Black Power came from physical strength, they looked as though they had it.

The weedheads in front of the pool hall north of 126th Street were the first to comment.

"Baby, them cats is full of pot," one said. "Make me high just to look at 'em."

"Baby, you is already high."

"Higher. But they so quiet. How come that?"

"How I know? Ask 'em."

"Hey, babies!" yelled the first weedhead. "Say something."

"You babies got any left?" yelled the second weedhead.

"Ignore those fools," the tallow man said.

"Come on, babies. Talk some black power language," the first weedhead cajoled.

A husky parader stepped out to reply. "I tells y'alls something, disgraceful dopefiends. I whip y'all's ass."

"Black Power!" a woman laughed.

"Thass right. I show 'em. I power their behinds."

"Be calm!" the tallow man admonished. "It's whitey what's the enemy."

"Stingy mothers!" the weedhead yelled. "Keep your old pot. It gonna cause your furnace to explode."

The people within earshot laughed, they were good-humored. It was all just a big joke. Three different kinds of protest parades.

"Like my Aunt Loo saying three bands play march music at my Uncle Boo's funeral," a soul sister said laughingly.

It was all really funny, in a grotesque way. The lynched Black Jesus who looked like a runaway slave. The slick-looking young man with his foreign white woman, riding in a car built for war service, preaching brotherhood. And last, but not least, these big Black Power people, looking strong and dangerous as religious fanatics, making black thunder and preaching Black Power.

Best show they'd had in a month of Sundays. Course the serious people frowned on these monkeyshines, but most citizens, out celebrating the day, were just amused.

Two big black men who looked as though they should have been with the Black Power marchers, instead sat watching them in the front seat of a small battered sedan parked at the curb in front of the African Memorial Bookstore. The small dirty black car looked out of place among all the shiny bright-colored cars out that night. And any two people doing nothing but sit on the sidelines and look, when there was so much to do that night, looked downright suspicious. What was more they wore dark suits and black slouch hats pulled so low they could barely be seen in the dim light filtering through the windshield, much less recognized unless one knew them. To the average incurious citizen they looked like two thugs waiting to stick up the jewelry store.

A slight dignified man standing beside them on the sidewalk volunteered, "These ain't all; there are two more."

"More what?" Coffin Ed asked.

"Parades."

Coffin Ed got out onto the sidewalk, and stood beside the little man, dwarfing him. Grave Digger got out from behind the wheel on the street side. They could see the parade coming up Seventh Avenue.

"Hell, that's a float," Grave Digger said.

At that moment Coffin Ed saw the old command car pass the corner of the jewelry store. "That ain't no float."

Grave Digger saw it and chuckled. "That's the general and his lady."

"Coffin Ed spoke to the little man beside him. "What's this carnival all about, Lomax?"

"It ain't no carnival."

"Well, what the hell is it then?" Grave Digger asked loudly from across the car. "It's your neighborhood. You're in with everything."

"I don't know these groups," Lomax said. "They ain't from around here. But they look serious to me."

"Serious? These clowns? You see more than I see."

"It ain't what I see. It's what I feel. I can feel they're serious. They ain't playing."

Coffin Ed grunted. Wordlessly Grave Digger clambered up the left fender and stood on the hood in order to see the parades more distinctly. He looked from the image of the lynched Black Jesus tied to the front of the Cadillac convertible to the face of the young man in the back of the old command car. He saw the first lines of the black and white marchers under the banner of Brotherhood. He saw the harelipped driver of the Cadillac and the laughing faces of the young black couples following beneath their banners of BLACK JESUS BABY. He looked at the leather-coated troopers across the street leading the Black Power procession. He heard Lomax exclaim excitedly, "They're gonna run head-on into each other."

Coffin Ed was climbing up the front fender on the other side. Fearing that the hood wouldn't hold them both, Grave Digger climbed on top of the body.

"What the hell's got into these people all of a sudden?" he heard Coffin Ed asking.

"It ain't been sudden," Lomax said. "They been feeling a long time. Like all the rest of us. Now they making their statement."

"Statement? Statement saying what?"

"Each of them got a different statement."

Grave Digger heard one of the leather-coated troopers shout, "Let's beat the shit out them sissies," and called down to Coffin Ed: "What they say is there's going to be some trouble if they start any shit. You better call the Lieutenant."

Ordinarily he would have shot into the air and waved his big pistol at the Black Power troopers, but they had strict orders not to draw their pistols in any circumstances except in the prevention of violent crime, the same as had been given to all the white cops.

Coffin Ed jumped down and climbed back inside. He couldn't get through to the precinct right away. In the meantime the two leather-coated troopers, followed by a group of hefty black men, had jumped over the concrete barrier around the park down the center of Seventh Avenue, and were racing toward the line of black and white youths approaching down 125th Street. Grave

Digger jumped to the ground and ran to head them off, throwing up his hands and yelling, "Get back! Straighten up!"

From the sidelines some comedian trumpeted, "Fly right!"

At the moment Coffin Ed got through to the Harlem precinct. "Lieutenant? It's me, Ed!"

Simultaneously the police cars began to move. Engines revved, sirens screamed. Seeing the police cars in action the people on the sidewalks began to scream and move into the street.

The metallic voice of Lieutenant Anderson rose into a scream. "I can't hear you. What's happening?"

"Call off the cops! The people are panicking!"

"What's that? I can't hear you. What's going on?"

Coffin Ed heard pandemonium breaking loose all around him, topped by the screaming of the police sirens.

"Call off the dogs!" he shouted.

"What's that? Everybody's calling. . . ."

"Call off the cops. . . ."

"What's that? What's all that noise? . . ."

"The white cops —"

"Work with the cops . . . keep calm. . . ."

". . . use our pistols . . . emergency. . . ."

". . . right . . . no pistols . . . keep order. . . ."

"ARE YOU DEAF?"

". . . COMMISSIONER . . . INSPECTOR . . . BE THERE. . . ."

"Hell's bells!" Coffin Ed muttered to himself, switched off the radio and leaped into the street. Down in the middle of the intersection he saw men rolling in the street like a free-for-all scramble. Two of them wore leather coats. One looked like Grave Digger. He broke in their direction.

Men from the Black Power parade were fistfighting in knots with the bare-limbed white and black youths from the Brotherhood. Several of them had surrounded the command car and dragged the two youths from the front seat. Others were trying to drag the white woman and colored man from the back seat. The young man was standing up kicking at their heads. The woman was lashing about with a wooden pole.

"Leave them biddies be," a fat woman was screaming.

"Whip they asses."

The white and black youths were fighting back side by side. Their opponents had the weight but they had the skill. The Black Power brothers were bulling ahead, but reaping black eyes and bloody noses on the way.

The mob of celebrants had overflowed into the street and stopped all the traffic. The police cars were stuck in a sea of sweating humanity. These people weren't taking sides in the main fight, they just wanted to chase the white cops. The cops were reluctant to leave their cars without the use of pistols.

Assisted by a group of laughing black girls, the harelipped man was endeavoring to drag the statue of the Black Jesus in the path of the police cars. But the cars couldn't move anyway and Jesus was slowly being dismembered in the crush of bodies. Shortly the crush had become so great, the police couldn't open the doors of their cars if they had wanted to. One rolled down his window and stuck his head out and was immediately swatted in the face by a woman's pocketbook.

The only fighting which showed any purpose was between the Black Power and the members of the Brotherhood. And when the Black Power fighters penetrated the defenses of the Brotherhood and came upon the interracial mob of followers, the result was a rout. They looked for sissies and prostitutes to beat. And they beat them with such abandon it looked indecent.

But the serious fighting was being done by Grave Digger and Coffin Ed against the leather-coated troopers, the silent clerics, and a number of other Black Power sluggers. The detectives had been down at first, but had taken advantage of their opponents, kicking to get their feet tangled up. They had got to their own feet, their clothes torn, noses bleeding, knots springing out from their heads and faces, and had begun fistfighting their opponents, back to back. Their long holstered pistols were exposed, but they had orders not to draw them. They couldn't have drawn them anyway, in the rain of fists showering over them. But they had one advantage. Every time a brother hit one of the pistols, his fist broke. They were hammering all right. But no one was falling down.

"One . . . " Grave Digger panted.

After an interval Coffin Ed echoed, "Two. . . . "

Instead of saying "three," they covered their heads with their hands and broke for the sidewalk, ploughing through a hail of fists. But once through, having gained the sidewalk in front of the jewelry store, no one tried to follow. Their opponents seemed satisfied with them out of the way, and turned their attention to the youths of the Brotherhood trying to protect the command car.

Lomax still stood beside their parked car. While watching the fight with interest he had been joined by a group of Black Muslims from the bookstore. They watched the detectives approach their car, noticing every detail of their appearance: swelling eyes, knotty heads, bruised faces, bloody noses, torn clothes, hard breathing and holstered pistols. Their eyes were fixed, their faces grave.

"Why the hell didn't you shoot?" Lomax said as they came abreast.

"You can't shoot people petitioning," Grave Digger said harshly, fishing a handkerchief from his pocket.

"Praise Allah," a Black Muslim said.

"Petitioning my ass," Lomax said. "All of them people are phoney."

"Funny," a Black Muslim said.

"That's a point of view," Grave Digger argued.

"Come on, let's beat it," Coffin Ed said. "Time's wasting."

But Lomax wanted to argue. "What point of view?"

"They want justice like everybody else," Grave Digger contended.

Lomax laughed derisively. "Long as you been in Harlem, you believe that shit. Do those clowns look like they're looking for justice?"

"For Christsake, Digger! You argue with this stooge," he shouted furiously, getting into his seat and slamming the door. "All he's trying to do is hold us."

Grave Digger hurried about the car and climbed beneath the wheel. "He's the people," he said defensively.

"Screw the people!" Coffin Ed said, adding: "And justice ain't the point. It's order now."

Before the car took off, Lomax called with sly malice, "Anyway, they beat the shit out of you."

"Don't let it fool you," Coffin Ed grated.

"We'll come up behind them," Grave Digger said, referring to the fighting groups.

The only traffic lane open was the one to the north. He had decided to drive north to 130th Street, which he thought would be open, then east to Park Avenue, and follow the railroad trestle back to 125th Street and approach Seventh Avenue from that direction.

But as he pulled away from the curb he caught sight in his rearview mirror of the command car being driven by the leader of the Brotherhood group running wild into the remnants of the Black Power group. It had pushed ahead with the engine racing north on the left side of Seventh Avenue, scattering the Black Power marchers, and had jumped the curb and ploughed through the midst of the spectators in front of the cigar store and was headed toward the plate-glass front of the pool hall and the fleeing weedheads. The white woman in the rear seat was clinging on for dear life.

But he and Coffin Ed had no way of going to their rescue. So he raced north and turned east into 130th Street on crying tires, hoping they'd get back in time. In the middle of the block between Seventh and Lenox Avenues they passed a panel delivery truck going in the same direction. They looked at it from force of habit and read the advertisement on the side: LUNATIC LYNDON . . . I DELIVER AND INSTALL TELEVISION SETS ANY TIME OF DAY OR NIGHT ANY PLACE Telephone Murray Hill 2. . . . Coffin Ed turned around to look at the license number, but he couldn't make it out in the dim street light. All he could see was that it was a Manhattan number.

"My people," he said. "Buying a television set in the middle of the night."

"Maybe the man's taking one back," Grave Digger said.

"The same thing."

"Hell, Lunatic ain't no fool. People got to work in the daytime to pay for them."

"I wasn't thinking about that. I was thinking night's the time for business in Harlem."

"Why not? They black, ain't they? White people do their dirt in the day. That's when they're most invisible."

Coffin Ed grunted.

The looting broke out on 125th Street at just the moment they were turning into Park Avenue beside the railroad trestle. The runaway command car had precipitated such confusion the white cops had struggled from their cars and begun shooting in the air. A number of adventuresome young men took advantage of the distraction and began breaking the store windows in the *Block* and snatching the first thing they could. Seeing them running with their arms filled with loot, the spectators stampeded in wild-eyed panic to get away from them.

13

"That's it. A mother-raping white man gets himself killed up here trying to get his kicks and here we are, two cops of the inferior race, stuck with trying to find out who killed him," Grave Digger held forth as he drove to the precinct that night in his private car.

"Too bad there ain't a mother-raping law against these freaks."

"Now, now, Ed, be tolerant. People call us freaks."

The grafted skin on Coffin Ed's face began to twitch. "Yeah, but not sex freaks."

"Hell, Ed, it ain't our business to worry about social morals," Grave Digger said placatingly, easing up on his friend. He knew folks called him a black Frankenstein, and he felt guilty because of it. If he hadn't been trying so hard to play tough the hoodlum would have never had a chance to throw the acid into Coffin Ed's face. "Leave 'em get dead."

The night before they had gone straight home from the Cozy

Flats and hadn't seen each other since. They didn't know what had happened to Lucas Covey, the building superintendent, whom they had beaten half to death.

"Anyway, the Acme folks probably got him out by now," Coffin Ed said in answer to their thoughts.

"Just as well, he'd done all his talking."

"John Babson! Hell, you think that's a name? I thought Covey was just blabbing."

"Maybe. Who knows?"

It was ten minutes to eight p.m. when they stopped in the detectives' locker room to change into their old black working coats. They found Lieutenant Anderson sitting at the Captain's desk, looking extremely worried as usual. Part of this was due to the fact that the Lieutenant was indoors so much his skin remained an unhealthy white, like that of a man who has been sick, and part due to the fact that Anderson's face was too sensitive for police work. But they were used to it. They knew the Lieutenant didn't worry as much as he seemed to, and that he was hip.

"It's a damn good thing the commissioner don't like pederasts," he greeted them.

Grave Digger looked sheepish. "Did the joint get steamed up?"

"It boiled over."

Coffin Ed was defiant. "Who was beefing?"

"The Acme Company's lawyers. They cried murder, brutality, anarchy, and everything else you can think of. They've filed charges with the police board of inquiry, and if they don't act they threaten to file a petition in the common pleas court."

"What the old man say?"

"Said he'd look into it, winking at the D.A."

"Woe is us," Grave Digger said. "Every time we brush a citizen gently with the tip of our knuckles, there's shysters on the sidelines to cry brutality, like a Greek chorus."

Anderson bowed his head to hide his smile. "You shouldn't play Theseus."

Grave Digger nodded in acknowledgement, but Coffin Ed's thoughts were on other matters.

"You'd think they'd want the killer caught," he said. "Being as the man was killed on their property."

"Who was he, anyway?" Grave Digger asked. "Did the boys downtown make him?"

"Yes, he was a Richard Henderson who had an apartment on lower Fifth Avenue, near Washington Square." Suddenly Anderson had become completely impersonal.

"Couldn't he find anything he wanted down there?" Coffin Ed put in.

"Married," Anderson continued as though he hadn't heard. "No children —"

"No wonder."

"A producer of new plays in off-Broadway theaters. For that, he had to have money."

"All the more reason they'd want to find his murderer," Grave Digger said thoughtfully.

"If by *they* , you mean the commissioner, the District Attorney and the courts, *they* do. It's the slum owners who're beefing. They don't want their employees killed in the process, it ain't worth it to them."

"Well, boss, it's as the French say, you can't make a ragout without cutting the meat."

"Well, that doesn't mean grinding it into beef hash."

"Ah, well, the more it's ground, the faster it cooks. I suppose our boy was well cooked?"

"Too well cooked. They took him out the pot. They got him out this morning on a writ of habeas corpus. I think they took him to a private hospital somewhere."

Both detectives looked at him solemnly. "You don't know where?" Grave Digger asked.

"If I knew, I wouldn't tell you. Lay off. For your own good. That boy spells trouble."

"What of it? Trouble is our business."

"Trouble for everyone."

"Oh, well, homicide will get him. They need him."

"Anyway, you can have a go at the other witnesses."

"Don't throw us no bones, boss. If any of those people picked up last night had known anything, they would have been to hell and gone away from there."

"Then you can have the men with the red fezzes."

"Lieutenant, let me tell you something. Most black men in Harlem who wear red fezzes are Black Muslims, and they're the most bitterly against this shit. Or else they're playing like they're Black Muslims, and they'd be risking their lives running down the street with a stolen pair of pants."

"Maybe, maybe not. Anyway, be discreet. Don't rake any more muck than necessary."

Grave Digger's neck began to swell and the tic went off in Coffin Ed's face.

"Listen, Lieutenant," Grave Digger said thickly. "This mother-raping white man gets himself killed on our beat chasing black sissies and you want us to whitewash the investigation."

Anderson's face got pink. "No, I don't want you to whitewash the investigation," he denied. "I just don't want you raking up manure for the stink."

"We got you; white men don't stink. You can depend on us, boss, we'll just go to the public gardens and watch the pansies bloom."

"Without manure," Coffin Ed said.

Nine p.m. found them sitting at the lunch counter in the Theresa building, watching the Harlem citizens pass along the intersection of Seventh Avenue and 125th Street.

"Two steak sandwiches," Grave Digger ordered.

The prissy brownskinned counterman with shiny conked curls gave them an all-inclusive look and batted his eyes. It was only two steps to the grill but he managed to swish on the way. He had a slender graceful neck, smooth brown arms and a wide ass in tight white jeans. He grilled two hamburgers and put them between two toasted buns on paper plates and placed them daintily before his customers. "Kraut or ketchup?" he asked seductively, lowering long black lashes over liquid brown eyes.

Grave Digger looked from the hamburgers to the counterman's lowered lashes. "I ordered steak sandwiches," he said belligerently.

The counterman fluttered his lashes. "This is steak," he said. "Ground steak."

"Steak in one piece."

The counterman regarded him appraisingly through the corners of his eyes.

"And I mean steak off the steer," Grave Digger added. "I ain't talking no doubletalk."

The counterman opened his eyes wide and looked straight into Grave Digger's eyes. "We don't have steak in one piece."

"Don't ask him," Coffin Ed cautioned out the corner of his mouth.

The counterman gave him a wide, white, scintillating smile. "I dig you," he murmured.

"Then dig up some ketchup and black coffee," Coffin Ed grated harshly.

Grave Digger winked at him as the counterman switched off. Coffin Ed looked disgusted.

"It wasn't a bad idea to call this Malcolm X Square," Grave Digger said aloud, to divert the counterman's attention.

"Could have just as well called it Khrushchev Place or Castro Corner," Coffin Ed replied, falling in with the maneuver.

"No, Malcolm X was a black man and a martyr to the black cause."

"You know one thing, Digger. He was safe as long as he kept hating the white folks — they wouldn't have hurt him, probably made him rich; it wasn't until he began including them in the human race they killed him. That ought to tell you something."

"It does. It tells me white people don't want to be included in a human race with black people. Before they'll be included they'll give 'em the whole human race. But it don't tell me who you mean by *they*."

"*They*, man, *they*. They'll kill you and me too if we ever stop being colored cops."

"I wouldn't blame them," Grave Digger said. "It'd bring about a hell of a lot of confusion." Noticing the counterman listening with rapt attention, he asked him, "What you think, Sugar Baby?"

The counterman lifted his upper lip and looked at him scornfully. "My name ain't Sugar Baby, I got a name."

"Well, what is it then?"

The counterman grinned slyly and said teasingly, "Don't you wish you knew?"

"Sweet as you are, what you need with a name?" Grave Digger needled.

"Don't hand me that shit. I know who you mother-rapers are. I'm here tending strictly to my own business."

"Good for you, Honey Baby; it'd be a damn sight better if everybody did that. But our business is to meddle into other people's business. That's why we're meddling into yours."

"Go ahead, I won't scream; see anything green, lick it up clean."

Grave Digger was stumped for the moment, but Coffin Ed took over for him.

"What Black Muslims eat here?"

The counterman was stumped. "Black Muslims?"

"Yeah, what Black Muslims you have as customers?"

"Those squares? They only eat their own food 'cause they claim all other food is dirty."

"You sure it ain't because they object to something else?"

"What do you mean by that?"

"It seems strange they wouldn't eat here when your food's so cheap and clean too."

The counterman didn't get it. He had a sneaking notion that Coffin Ed meant something else and he frowned angrily because he didn't understand and turned away. He went down the counter to serve a customer on the 125th Street side. There were only three of them at the counter, but he stayed away from the two detectives. He looked into the faces of the passing people; he stared at the passing traffic. Then suddenly he switched back and placed himself directly in their faces and put his hands on his hips and looked straight into Coffin Ed's eyes.

"It ain't that, it's their religion," he said.

"What?"

"Black Muslims."

"That's right. You must see a lot of jokers who look like Black Muslims."

"Sure." He raised his gaze and nodded toward the bookstore diagonally across the street. Several black men wearing red fezzes were gathering on the sidewalk. "There're some now."

Coffin Ed glanced around and looked back. "We don't want those, we're looking for fakes."

"Fake what?"

"Fake Muslims."

The counterman broke into sudden laughter. His long-lashed eyes regarded them indulgently. "You policemen, you don't know what you want. Coffee? Pie? Ice cream?"

"We got coffee."

The counterman pouted. "You want some more?"

Their attention was diverted by two women in a foreign sports car that turned the corner from 125th Street and passed at a crawl south on Seventh Avenue. Both were large amazonian types with strong bold features and mannish-cut hair. Their brownskinned faces were handsome. The one driving wore a man's shirt of green crêpe de chine and a yellow silk knitted tie; while the other one beside her wore a sun-back dress without shoulder straps and the front so low she looked stark naked sitting there. They stared in the direction of the lunch counter.

"Friends of yours?" Grave Digger asked.

"Those queers?"

"Didn't look queer to me. One was a man; a good-looking man at that."

"Man my ass, they were lesbos."

"How do you know? You been out with them?"

"Don't be insulting. I don't associate with those kind of people."

"No Beaux Arts ball? No garden parties?"

The counterman curled his upper lip. He was good at it. "You're so crude," he said.

"Where's everybody?" Coffin Ed asked to get Grave Digger out of trouble.

Willing to call quits, the counterman replied soberly, "It's always slack at this time."

But Coffin Ed wouldn't let him off. "That ain't what I mean."

The counterman stared at him hostilely. "What do you mean, then?"

"You know, *everybody*."

Then suddenly the counterman flew coy. "I'm here," he cooed. "Ain't that enough?"

"Enough for what?"

"Don't play square."

"You're forgetting we're policemen."

"I like policemen."

"Ain't you scared?"

"Why, I ain't been caught."

"Policemen are brutes."

The counterman raised his eyebrows superciliously. "I beg your pardon?"

"BRUTES!"

"You're just fanning his interest," Grave Digger said.

He looked at Grave Digger with a smirk. "You know everything, tell me what I'm thinking?"

"When do you get off work?" Grave Digger countered.

His eyelashes fluttered uncontrollably as he went all unnecessary. "Twelve o'clock."

"Then you weren't here last night after twelve?"

His face fell. "You sadistic son of a bitch!"

"So you couldn't have seen Jesus Baby when he stopped by?"

"Come again?"

"*Jesus Baby*?"

Neither detective caught a flicker of recognition in his demeanor. "Jesus Baby? That someone?"

"A friend of yours."

"Not mine, I don't know no one named Jesus Baby."

"Sure you do. You're just scared to admit it."

"Oh, *Him*! I love *Him*. And he loves me too."

"I'm sure of it."

"I'm religious."

"All right, all right, now cut out the bullshit. You know exactly who we mean. The colored one. The one who lives right here in Harlem."

They noticed a subtle change in his manner but they couldn't tell what it meant. "Oh, *him*?"

They waited suspiciously. It was coming too easy.

"You mean the one who lives on 116th Street? You don't go for him, do you?"

"Where on 116th Street?"

"Where?" The counterman tried to look hip. "You know where. That little door beside the movie; between it and the lunch counter. You kidding me?"

"What floor?"

"You just go straight on through. You'll find him."

They had a strong suspicion they were being taken, but there wasn't any choice.

"What's his straight name?"

"Straight name? *Jesus Baby*, that's all."

"If we don't find him, we'll be back," Coffin Ed threatened.

The counterman gave him his most seductive smile. "Oh, you'll find him. And give him my love. But come back, anyway."

They found the door all right just where he had said; it was the entrance to a tenement six storeys high, the iron fire escape along the front descending to the plate-glass window of the luncheonette where pork ribs were barbecuing before an electric grill. But they overcame the temptation and went inside. They found the usual tenement hall, walls scratched with graffiti, urine stink coming up from the floor, food and last week's air. The hall led to The Temple of the Black Jesus. Hanging by the neck from the rotting plaster ceiling of a large square room was a gigantic plaster of paris image of the Black Jesus. There was an expression of teeth-bared rage on the black face. The arms were spread, the hands were balled into fists, the toes were curled. Black plaster blood dripped from red-pointed nail holes. The legend underneath read: THEY LYNCHED ME.

They went inside. A man stood inside the doorway examining the people who entered and collecting the price of admission. He was a short, fat, black man with a harelip. Sweat ran from his face as though his skin were leaking. His short black hair grew so thick on his round inflated head it looked like nylon pile. His body looked blown up like that of a rubber man. The sky-blue suit he wore glinted like metal.

"Two dollars," he said.

Grave Digger gave him two dollars and went ahead.

He stopped Coffin Ed. "Two dollars."

"My friend paid."

"That's right. That was for him. Now two dollars for you." Spit sprayed when he spoke.

Coffin Ed backed away and gave the man two dollars.

Inside there was so little light and so much unrelieved blackness in the walls, the people's clothes, their skins, their hair, they could only distinguish the white crescents of eyes, hanging in the dark like op art. And then they saw the metallic glitter of the hairlipped man as he took the rostrum and began to harangue: "Now we're gonna feed him the flesh of the Black Jesus until he choke —"

"Jesus baby!" someone cried. "I hear you!"

" 'Cause I doan have to tell you the flesh of Jesus is indigestible," the metallic man went on. " 'Cause they ain't even digested the flesh of the white Jesus in these two thousand years, an' they been eating him every Sunday. . . ."

They turned around and went back the way they had come. Because they had time to kill before midnight, they stopped at the lunch counter and had two servings of barbecue apiece, with coleslaw and potato salad.

It was midnight when they returned to the lunch counter in Malcolm X Square and the scene had changed. The street was filled with people from the late show at the Apollo and the double feature at Leow's and RKO. The streets were crowded with motor traffic, going all ways. The lunch counter was filled with hungry people, men and women, couples, straight people who wanted to eat. There was an additional counterman on duty and two darkskinned waitresses. The waitresses looked evil, but there wasn't anything queer about them but their reasons for looking evil because they had to work. The new counterman looked prissy, too, and they would have liked to talk to him but their counterman spotted them and came over and stood before them with one hand on his hip. He was going off duty and had already taken off his apron and unbuttoned his white coat so that his breasts were almost showing. He licked his lips and fluttered his eyelashes and smiled. They noticed he had already applied some tan lipstick.

"Did you find him all right?" he asked sweetly.

"Sure, just like you said," Grave Digger replied.

"Did you give him my love?"

"We couldn't. We forgot to get your name."

"That was too bad. I didn't tell it to you."

"Tell us now, baby? Your straight name? The one you have to give to policemen who don't like you."

He blinked his eyes. "Oooo, don't you like me?"

"Sure we like you. That's why we came back."

"John Babson," he said coyly.

The detectives froze.

"John Babson!" Coffin Ed echoed.

"Well, John Babson, baby, put on your prettiest panties," Grave Digger said. "You got company, honey."

14

The panel delivery truck drew up before the front of the "Amsterdam Apartments" on 126th Street between Madison and Fifth Avenues. Words on its sides, barely discernible in the dim street light, read: LUNATIC LYNDON . . . I DELIVER AND INSTALL TELEVISION SETS ANY TIME OF DAY OR NIGHT ANY PLACE.

Two uniformed delivery men alighted and stood on the sidewalk to examine an address book in the light of a torch. Dark faces were highlighted for a moment like masks on display and went out with the light. They looked up and down the street. No one was in sight. Houses were vague geometrical patterns of black against the lighter blackness of the sky. Crosstown streets were always dark.

Above them, in the black squares of windows, crescent-shaped whites of eyes and quarter moons of yellow teeth bloomed like Halloween pumpkins. Suddenly voices bubbled in the night.

"Lookin' for somebody?"

The driver looked up. "Amsterdam Apartments."

"These is they."

Without replying, the driver and his helper began unloading a wooden box. Stenciled on its side were the words: Acme Television "Satellite" A.406.

"What that number?" someone asked.

"Fo-o-six," Sharp-eyes replied.

"I'm gonna play it in the night house if I ain't too late."

"What ya'll got there, baby?"

"Television set," the driver replied shortly.

"Who dat getting a television this time of night?"

The delivery man didn't reply.

A man's voice ventured, "Maybe it's that bird liver on the third storey got all them mens."

A woman said scornfully, "Bird liver! If she bird liver I'se fish and eggs and I got a daughter old enough to has mens."

" . . . or not!" a male voice boomed. "What she got 'ill get television sets when you jealous old hags is fighting over mops and pails."

"Listen to the loverboy! When yo' love come down last?"

"Bet loverboy ain't got none, bird liver or what."

"Ain't gonna get none either. She don't burn no coal."

"Not in dis life, next life maybe."

"You people make me sick," a woman said from a group on the sidewalk that had just arrived. "We looking for the dead man and you talking 'bout tricks."

The two delivery men were silently struggling with the big television box but the new arrivals got in their way.

"Will you ladies kindly move your asses and look for dead men sommers else," the driver said. His voice sounded mean.

" 'Scuse me," the lady said. "You ain't got him, is you?"
"Does I look like I'm carrying a dead man 'round in my pocket?"
"Dead man! What dead man? What you folks playing?" a man called down interestedly. "Skin?"
"Georgia skin? Where?"
"Ain't nobody playing no skin," the lady said with disgust. "He's one of us."
"Who?"
"The dead man, that's who."
"One of usses? Where he at?"
"Where he at? He dead, that's where he at."
"Let me get some green down on dead man's row."
"Ain't you the mother's gonna play fo-o-six?"
"Thass all you niggers thinks about," the disgusted lady said. "Womens and hits!"
"What else is they?"
"Where yo' pride? The white cops done killed one of usses and thass all you can think about."
"Killed 'im where?"
"We don't know where. Why you think we's looking?"
"You sho' is a one-tracked woman. I help you look, just don't call me nigger is all."
The delivery men had got the box halfway up the front steps and had stopped to get their breath. "We could use a little help," the driver said. "Being as you're spreading it around."
No one really believed in the dead man, but the television set was real. A big burly brother clad in blue denim overalls stepped from the ground-floor window. "All right. I'll help. I'm the super. Where she go?"
"Third-storey front. Miss Barbara Tynes."
"I said it!" a woman cried triumphantly.
"Why ain't you gettin' one then?" the scornful woman said. "You got the same thing she is?"
"He-he, must not have," a new female voice observed.
"Leave my ol' lady be," a man's voice grumbled from the dark. "She get everything she need."

"Says you."

A slim silhouette in a luminous white shirt emerged from the dark entrance hall. "I'll give you a hand." Hair like burnished metal gleamed on an egg-shaped head.

"You sniffing at the wrong tuft, Slick, baby," said a sly female voice from somewhere above. "She like chalk."

"We got some'pm in common then," Slick said.

"All right, mens, all together now," the driver said, putting his weight to the box.

The four men slid it up the front stairs and lifted it over the sill into the front hall.

The big burly super was the first to complain. "This here set must be made of solid lead."

"You been doing too much night work," the driver joked.

"Yo' old lady taken yo' strength."

"Maybe it ain't a television set, maybe it's gold bars," a spectator cracked. "Maybe her business is booming."

"Let's open it and see," suggested some unseen agitator.

"We gonna open it when we get it up, and all of youse can see it," the driver said. "We got an old one to take back."

"I declare, I never heard of such a thing, changing television sets in the middle of the night." The woman sounded as though personally affronted.

"Ain't it a sin?" someone needled.

"I ain't said that," the woman denied. "Who she getting it from anyway?"

"Lunatic Lyndon," the driver replied.

"No wonder," the woman said in a mollified voice. "Delivering a new set up here in Harlem this time of the night."

The elevator was out of order, as usual, and the four men had to carry the heavy box up the stairs, sweating and grunting and cursing, with the curious spectators trailing behind like they expected to see a phenomenon.

"Whew! Let's set it down for a while," Slick said when they reached the first landing. He looked around at the gaping followers and sneered with contempt. "You people! A man can't open his fly in this town before you nosy people crowding about to see what he gonna pull out."

A man chuckled. "Can you blame us? He might pull out a knife."

"We're ranking Slick's play," another man said.

"Well, I ain't got no knife in mine," Slick said.

A woman sniggered. "Better had. Where you going?"

"If he 'spects to do any cuttin'," the second man cracked.

The woman from the street who had announced she was looking for the dead man spoke up. "Here you niggers is talking under y'all's clothes when there is one of usses laying dead somewheres."

"Aw, woman, look in the undertaker's, thass where dead mens is."

"That woman needs a live man to shut her up."

"Good an' alive."

"All right, buddies, let's go," the driver said encouragingly, attacking the heavy box like it was a Japanese wrestler. "All this confabulating ain't getting us nowhere."

"Listen to the 'fessor sling that jawbreaker."

But the suggestion of a superior intelligence quieted them for a moment and by then they'd got the box to moving again. When they'd got it into the third-storey hall, the driver checked his delivery book again.

"It'd be funny if he got the wrong address," a woman said.

Ignoring her, the driver rapped on an oakstained door.

"Who is it?" a female voice asked from within.

"Lunatic Lyndon. We got a television set for Miss Barbara Tynes."

"That's me," the voice admitted. "Just wait a minute while I put something on."

"You don't need to," a male spectator said.

A laugh tinkled inside. Grins broke out.

"Get yo' knife ready, Slick, baby," someone said.

"It stay ready," Slick said.

"All right, folks, gather 'bout," the driver said. "We gonna open her and look for them gold bars."

"I was just joking," the gold-bar man backtracked.

The driver gave him an evil look. "Damn right. Like half the people in the cemeteries."

The top of the box was stenciled: THIS SIDE UP. The driver took a short crowbar from beneath his uniform and pried off the boards on the side facing the spectators. A dark glass screen was revealed.

"That a television set?" the big burly super exclaimed. "It look more like the front of a bank."

"She get tired of looking at it she can go inside it and look out," a spectator said.

The delivery men looked as proud as though they'd produced a miracle. All thoughts of a dead man were forgotten.

The lock clicked in the oakstained door. The door began to open. Everyone looked. The red-nailed fingers of a woman's hand held the door open. The head of a woman peered around the edge. It was the head of a young woman with a smooth brownskinned face and straightened black hair pulled tightly aslant her forehead over her right eye. It was a good-looking face with a wide, thick unpainted mouth with brown lips. Brown eyes, magnified behind rimless spectacles, became larger still at sight of the gaping spectators. From her side she couldn't see into the box; the screen was not visible to her. All she saw was the boarding on the floor and the leering man.

"My TeeVee!" she exclaimed and pitched forward onto the green carpeted floor. The pink silk robe, pulled tight about her voluptuous hips, hiked up from the smooth brown length of legs to show a heavy patch of curly black hair.

Eyes bugged.

The delivery men leaped into the room and pounced on her like vicious dogs on a juicy bone.

"Heart attack!" the driver shouted.

The spectators winced.

"Give her air!" the helper cried.

The spectators surged pell-mell into the room.

A long sofa stretched across the front window. A glass-topped cocktail table sat in front of it. On one side was an armchair. On the other a white-oak television stand. Out in the center of the room was a deal table with four straight-backed chairs. Floor lamps stood about, all lit. A man's straw hat lay on the sofa, but no man was in sight. Four other doors led somewhere, but all were closed.

"Somebody call a doctor!" the driver cried.

The spectators looked about for a telephone, none was in view.

"Where the hell is the medicine cabinet?" the helper asked in a panic-stricken voice like a peacemaker at sight of a cut throat.

The spectators rushed about to look. They found all doors but the front door locked.

Only the big burly super had the presence of mind to ask, "What you take for these attacks, lady?"

The others were too busy looking at her crotch.

Maybe she heard him. Maybe she didn't. But suddenly she gasped, "Whiskey!"

Relief fell over the assemblage. If whiskey could save her, she was saved. In a matter of minutes the room looked like a whiskey store.

She clutched the first bottle she saw and drank from the neck as though it were water. Her face took on a different expressions, one after another, then she gasped, "My TeeVee? It's bursted."

"No, mam!" the driver cried. "Oh, no, mam, it ain't busted. I just opened it."

"Opened it? Opened my TeeVee. I'm going to call the police. Somebody call the police."

The spectators melted away. Maybe they went for the police. Maybe they didn't. One minute the room was filled with them. Offering her whiskey. Staring at her crotch. The women for comparison. The men for other reasons. The next minute they were gone.

Only she and the delivery men were left. The delivery men closed and locked the door. A half-hour later they unlocked and opened the door. They began to take away the wooden television box. It had been boarded up again. One was at the front and one at the back. It didn't seem any lighter than before. They staggered beneath the weight.

No one came to help them. No one appeared to look. No one appeared at all. The upstairs hall was empty. The staircase was empty. The downstairs hall was empty. They encountered no one on the sidewalk or on the street. They didn't seem surprised. The word *police* has the power of magic in Harlem. It can make whole houses filled with people disappear.

15

"Sit down between us, baby," Grave Digger said, patting the seat beside him.

John Babson looked from him to the towering figure of Coffin Ed beside him, and said playfully, "This is sociable, it isn't an arrest?" He was resplendent in a long-sleeved white silk shirt with a Russian collar and glove-tight skin-colored cotton satin pants that glowed like naked skin. He didn't think for a moment it was an arrest.

Grave Digger eyed him interestedly from behind the wheel.

"Go on, get in," Coffin Ed urged, taking his arm like he would a woman's. "You said you liked policemen."

He got in exactly like a woman and moved close to Grave Digger to make room for Coffin Ed.

"Because if it is, I want to call my lawyer," he continued with his little joke.

Grave Digger paused in the act of pressing the starter button. "You got a lawyer?"

He was tired of it. "The company has."

"Who?"

"Oh, I don't know. I haven't ever needed him."

"You don't need him now, unless you prefer his company."

"He's an ofay."

"Don't you like ofays?"

"I like y'all better."

"You'll like us even better later on," Grave Digger said, starting the car.

"Where y'all taking me?"

"A place you know."

"You can come to my place."

"This *is* your place." He drove to the front of the building where the white man had been killed.

Coffin Ed got out on to the sidewalk and reached in to help John out. But he drew back against Grave Digger in alarm.

"This *isn't* my place," he protested. "What kind of place is this?"

"Go on and get out," Grave Digger said, pushing him. "You'll like it."

Looking puzzled and curious, he let Coffin Ed pull him to the sidewalk.

"It's a basement," Coffin Ed said, taking his arm as Grave Digger came around the car and took his other arm.

He shook himself but he didn't struggle. "How about this!" he exclaimed softly. "Is it clean?"

"Be quiet now," Grave Digger whispered suggestively as they walked him down the narrow, slanting alleyway to the green door halfway down. They found the door locked and sealed.

"It's locked," John whispered.

"Shhhh!" Grave Digger cautioned.

A voice from an open window in the building next door whispered hoarsely, "You niggers better get away from there. The police is watching you."

John stiffened suddenly with suspicion. "What you trying to do to me?"

"Ain't this your room?" Coffin Ed asked.

The whites of John's eyes showed suddenly in the dark. "My room? I live on Hamilton Terrace. I ain't never seen this place."

"Our error," Grave Digger said, holding firmly to his arm. He could feel the trembling of his body coming through his arm.

"Maybe he'll like the Cozy Flats," Coffin Ed said. He intended to sound persuasive, instead he sounded sinister.

John's excitement suddenly left him. He felt deflated and a little scared. He was finished with the adventure.

"I ain't interested," he said crossly. "Just let me alone."

"Leave that boy alone," the voice from the darkened window said. "You come with me, baby, I'll protect you."

"I ain't interested in none of you mother-rapers," John said, his voice rising. "Just take me back where you got me."

"Come on then," Grave Digger said, steering him back to the sidewalk.

"I thought you said you liked us," Coffin Ed said, bringing up the rear.

John felt safer back on the sidewalk and he tried to shake himself loose from Grave Digger's grip. His voice was louder too.

"I ain't said no such thing. What you take me for? I ain't that way."

Grave Digger turned him over to Coffin Ed and went around the car.

"Just get in," Coffin Ed said, applying a little force.

Grave Digger slid beneath the wheel and reached over and pulled him down on to the seat. "Don't struggle, baby," he said. "We're just going to drive by the Cozy Flats and then we'll take you home."

"Where you can feel relaxed," Coffin Ed added, pushing in beside him.

"I don't want to go to the Cozy Flats," John screamed. "Leave me out here. Do you think I'm gay? I ain't gay —"

"Merry then."

"I'm straight. I just got a happy disposition. Girls like me. I ain't queer. You're making a mistake."

"What are you getting so hysterical about?" Grave Digger said hotly, as though he were annoyed. "What's the matter with you? What you got against the Cozy Flats? Is there somebody there you don't want to see?"

"I ain't never heard of the Cozy Flats, nor nobody lives there, far as I know. And turn me loose, you're hurting me."

Grave Digger started the car and drove off.

"I'm sorry," Coffin Ed said, letting go his arm. "It's just because I'm so strong."

"You ain't exciting me," John said scornfully.

Grave Digger brought the car to a stop in front of the Cozy Flats.

"Recognize this place?" Coffin Ed asked.

"I ain't never seen it."

"Lucas Covey is the super."

"What about it? I don't know no Lucas Covey."

"He knows about you."

"Lots of people know me who I don't know."

"I'll bet."

"He said he rented you the room," Grave Digger said.

"What room?"

"The one we just left."

"You mean that basement what was locked up?" He looked from one hard black face to the other one. "What's this? A frame? I should'a known there was something wrong with you mother-rapers. I got a right to call my lawyer."

"You don't know his name," Grave Digger reminded him.

"I'll just call the personnel office."

"There ain't nobody there this time of night."

"You dirty sadistic bastards!"

"Don't lose your pretty ways. We got nothing against you, personally. It was Lucas Covey who told us about you. He said he rented the room to a seal-brown young man named John Babson. He said John Babson was beautiful and sweet. That describes you."

"Don't hand me that shit," John said, but he preened with pleasure. "You're making that up. I ain't never heard of nobody named Lucas Covey. You take me in and I'll confront him."

"I thought you didn't want to go inside," Coffin Ed said. "With us, anyway."

"Maybe by another name," Grave Digger said.

"Why can't I confront him?"

"He ain't there."

"What's he look like?"

"Slender black man with narrow face and egg-shaped head. West Indian."

"I don't know nobody like that."
"Don't lie, baby, I saw the recognition in your eyes."
"Shit! You see everything in my eyes."
"Ain't you pleased?"
"But the man you described could be anybody."
"This one is gay, like you."
"Don't make a fool out of yourself; I told you, I ain't gay."
"All right, but we know you know this man."
John became appealing. "What can I do to convince you?"
"I thought you said you weren't gay."
"I didn't mean that."
"All right, let's negotiate."
"Negotiate how?"
"Like the East and the West. We want information."
John grinned and forgot to be bitchy. "You're the West then; what do I get?"
"There's two of us, you get double the price."
He broke up as though he would cry. Every time he tried to play straight they wouldn't let him. He would succumb to desire, but he wasn't sure. It all left him frustrated and a little frightened.
"Shit on both of you, you sadistic mother-rapers," he said.
"Listen, baby, we want to know about this man, and if you don't tell us, we'll whip your ass."
"Don't excite him," Coffin Ed cautioned. "He'd like that." Turning to John, he said, "Get this, pretty boy, I'll knock out your pretty white teeth and gouge your bedroom eyes out of shape. When I get through with you, you'll be known as the ugly fairy."
John got truly frightened. He put his hands between his legs and squeezed them. His voice was pleading. "I don't know nothing, I swear. You bring me here to places I ain't never seen, and ask me about a man I ain't never heard of who looks like anybody—"
"Richard Henderson, then?"
John broke off in mid-speech and his mouth hung open.
"I see that name scored."
He was ludicrous trying to get himself together. He couldn't follow the sudden switch. He didn't know whether to be relieved

or terrified; whether to admit he knew him or deny all acquaintance.

"Er, you mean Mr Henderson, the producer?"

"That's the one, the white producer who likes pretty colored boys."

"I don't know him that well. All I know about him is he produces plays. I had a part in a play he produced on downtown Second Avenue called *Pretty People*."

"I'll bet you were the lead."

He smiled secretly.

"Just wipe that smirk off your face and tell us where we can find him."

"At his home, I suppose. He's got a wife."

"We don't want to see his wife. Where does he hang out by himself?"

"Any place in the Village, although this time of night he might be somewhere on St Marks Place."

"Where else is there on St Marks Place except The Five Spot?"

"Oh, plenty places for the cognoscenti, you just got to know where they are."

"All right, you show us."

"When?"

"Now."

"Now? I can't. I got to go home."

"You got someone waiting?"

He fluttered his lashes and looked coy again. He had beautiful eyes and he knew it. "Always," he said.

"Then we'll have to kidnap you," Grave Digger said.

"And keep your mother-raping hands away from me," Coffin Ed snarled.

"Square!" he said contemptuously.

They drove down through Central Park and turned over to Third Avenue on 59th Street, passing first the exclusive high-rent, high-living district around 59th Street and Fifth Avenue, and then the arty, chichi section of antique shops, French restaurants, expensive pederasts on Third Avenue in the fifties and upper forties until they reached the wide, black, smooth paved expanse that passed through Cooper Square, and they had come to the end of their journey. They remembered the days of the Third Avenue elevated, the dark cobblestoned street underneath, where the Bowery bums pissed on passing cars at night, but neither spoke about it for fear of distracting John from the strange, glittering excitement that had overcome him. As far as they could see, St Marks Place itself was no cause for excitement. Externally, it was as dreary a street as one could find, unchanged, dirty, narrow, sinister-looking. It was the continuation of 8th Street, which ran between Third and Second Avenues. On the west side, between Fifth and Sixth Avenues, 8th Street was the heart of Greenwich Village, and Richard Henderson had lived in the new luxury apartments on the corner of Fifth Avenue. But St Marks Place was something else again.

Jazz joint on one corner, open for business, The Five Spot. Delicatessen on the other, closed, beer cans in the window. White Mercedes drives up before The Five Spot, white-coated white woman with shining white hair driving. Black man beside her with bebop beard, clown's hat. Kisses her, gets out. Goes into The Five Spot. She drives away. "Rich white bitch . . ." John mutters. On other corner in front of beer cans in delicatessen window, two black boys in blue jeans, gray sneakers, black shirts. Faces pitted with smallpox scars. Hair nappy. Teeth white. Faces scarred from razor slashes. Cotton hair, matted, unkempt. All young, early twenties. Three white girls looking like spaceage witches. Young girls. In their teens. Witches are children in this age. Long unkempt dark brown hair. Hanging down. Dirty faces. Dark eyes. Slack mouths. Stained black jeans. All moving in slow motion, as though drugged. It made the detectives feel woozy just looking at them.

"Who was your daddy, blacky boy?" a white girl asks.

"My daddy is a cracker," the black boy answers. "But he got a job for me."

"On his plantation," the white girl says.

"Ole massa McBird!" the black boy says.

They all burst into loud unrestrained laughter.

"Wanna go to The Five Spot?" John asked.

"You think he's in there?" Grave Digger asked, thinking, *If he is, he's a mother-raping ghost.*

"Richard goes there sometimes, but it's early for him."

"Richard? If you know him all that well, why don't you call him Dick?"

"Oh, Dick sounds so vulgar."

"Well, where else does he go, by any name?"

"He meets people all around. He picks up lots of actors for his plays."

"I ain't a damn bit surprised," Grave Digger said, then pointed to a building next to The Five Spot, asked: "What about that hotel there? You know it?"

"The Alicante? Home away from it all? Nobody lives there but junkies, prostitutes, pushers and maybe some Martians too from the looks of them."

"Henderson ever go there?"

"I don't know why. Nobody there he'd want to see."

"No *Pretty People*, eh? He wasn't on the shit?"

"Not as far as I know of. He just took a trip now and then."

"How about you?"

"Me? I don't even drink."

"I mean have you ever been there?"

"Goodness no."

"It figures."

John grinned and slapped him on the leg.

Next to it in the direction of Second Avenue was a steam-bath establishment calling itself the Arabian Nights Baths.

"That a fish bowl?"

John batted his eyes but didn't reply.

"Does he go there?"

He shrugged.

"All right, let's go see if he's there."

"I better warn you," he said. "The markees are there."

"You mean maquis," Grave Digger corrected. "M-a-q-u-i-s."

"No, markees, m-a-r-q-u-i-s-e. Bite each other!"

"Well, well, that is what they do? Bite each other?"

John giggled.

They went up steps from the street and passed through a short narrow hall lit by a bare fly-specked bulb. A fat, greasy-faced man sat behind a counter in a cage at the front of the locker room. He wore a soiled white shirt without a collar from which the sleeves had been torn, sweat-stained suspenders attached to faded, stained seersucker pants big enough to fit an elephant. His head went down in sweat-wet folds of fat into a lump of blubber with arms. His face was only black-rimmed thick lenses holding magnified cooked eyes.

He put three keys on the counter. "Put your clothes in your locker. Got any valuables, better leave them with me."

"We just want a look," Grave Digger said.

The fat man rolled cooked eyes at John's getup. "You got to get naked."

John's hand flew to his mouth as though he were shocked.

"You don't understand me," Grave Digger said. "We're the law. Policemen. Detectives. See?" He and Coffin Ed flashed their shields.

The fat man was unimpressed.

"Policemen are my best customers."

"I'll bet."

They meant different things.

"Tell me who you looking for; I know everybody in there."

"Dick Henderson," John Babson said.

"Jesus Baby," Grave Digger said.

The fat man shook his head. The detectives moved toward the steam room.

John hesitated. "I'll take off my clothes, I don't want to spoil them." He looked from one detective to the other. "It won't take but a minute."

"We don't want to lose you," Grave Digger said.

"Which might happen if you show your shape," Coffin Ed added.

John pouted. In the familiar scene he felt he could say what he wished. "Old meanies."

Naked bodies came out of white steam as thick as fog; fat bodies and lean bodies, black bodies and white bodies, scarcely different except in color. Eyes stared resentfully at the clothed figures.

"What they do with the chains?" Grave Digger asked.

"You're awfully square for a policeman."

"I've always heard it was twigs."

"That must have been before the markees."

If John saw anyone whom he knew, he didn't let on. The detectives didn't expect to recognize anyone. Back on the sidewalk, they stood for a moment looking down toward Second Avenue. On the corner was a sign advertising ice cream and chocolate candies. But next door was a darkened plate-glass front of some kind of auditorium. Cards in the windows announced that Martha Schlame was singing Israeli Folk Songs and Bertolt Brecht.

"The Gangler Circus is generally here," John said.

"Circus?"

"You got a dirty mind," John accused. "And it ain't the kind with lions and elephants either. It's just the Gangler Brothers and a dog, a rooster, a donkey and a cat. They got a red and gold caravan they travel in."

"Leave them to the sprouts and let's finish with this," Coffin Ed said impatiently.

Down here the people were different from the people in Harlem. Even the soul brothers. They looked more lost. People in Harlem seem to have some purpose, whether good or bad. But the people down here seemed to be wandering around in a daze, lost, without knowing where they were or where they were going. Moving in slow motion. Dirty and indifferent. Uncaring and unwashed. Rejecting reality, rejecting life.

"This makes Harlem look like a state fair," Grave Digger said.

"Makes us look like we're from the country too."

"Feel like it anyway."

They crossed the street and went back down the other side, coming abreast a big wooden building painted red with green trimmings. The sign over the entrance read: *Dom Polsky Nardowy*.

"What's this fire hazard, sonny?"

"That horror? That's the Polish National Home."

"For old folks?"

"All I ever seen there was Gypsies," John confessed, adding after a moment: "I dig Gypsies."

Suddenly they were all three fed up with the street. By common consent they crossed over to The Five Spot.

Interlude

"I take it you've discovered who started the riot," Anderson said.

"We knew who he was all along," Grave Digger said.

"It's just nothing we can do to him," Coffin Ed echoed.

"Why not, for God's sake?"

"He's dead," Coffin Ed said.

"Who?"

"Lincoln," Grave Digger said.

"He hadn't ought to have freed us if he didn't want to make provisions to feed us," Coffin Ed said. "Anyone could have told him that."

"All right, all right, lots of us have wondered what he might have thought of the consequences," Anderson admitted. "But it's too late to charge him now."

"Couldn't have convicted him anyway," Grave Digger said.

"All he'd have to do would be to plead good intentions," Coffin Ed elaborated. "Never was a white man convicted as long as he plead good intentions."

"All right, all right, who's the culprit this night, here, in Harlem? Who's inciting these people to this senseless anarchy?"

"Skin," Grave Digger said.

16

From where they sat, the rioting looked like a rehearsal for a modern ballet. The youths would surge suddenly from the dark tenement doorways, alleyways, from behind parked cars and basement stairways, charge towards the police, throw rotten vegetables, and chunks of dirt, and stones and bricks if they could find them, and some rotten eggs, but not too many because an egg had to be good and rotten before it went for bad in Harlem; taunting the police, making faces, sticking out their tongues, chanting, "Drop dead, whitey!" Their bodies moving in grotesque rhythm, lithe, lightfooted, agile and fluid, charged with a hysterical excitement that made them look unhealthily animated.

The sweating, red-faced cops in their blue uniforms and white helmets slashed the hot night air with their long white billies as though dancing a cop's version of *West Side Story*, and ducked from the flying missiles, chiefly to keep the dirt out of their eyes; then it was their turn and they chased the black youths who turned and fled easily back into the darkness.

Spokesmen from the 125th Street offices of the NAACP and CORE were mounted on Police Department sound trucks appealing to the youths to go home, saying their poor unhappy parents would have to pay. Only the white cops paid any attention. The Harlem youths couldn't care less.

"It's just a game to them," Coffin Ed said.

"No, it ain't," Grave Digger contradicted. "They're making a statement."

While the police were diverted momentarily to a group of boys and girls launching a harassment on 125th Street, a gang of older youths charged from the shadows toward a supermarket in the middle of the block with beer bottles and scraps of iron. The glass shattered. The youths began darting in to loot, like sparrows snitching crumbs from under the beaks of larger birds.

Coffin Ed looked sideways at Grave Digger. "What's that statement say?"

Grave Digger straightened in his seat. It was the first time either of them had moved. He noticed the red-faced white cops turn in that direction. "Says there's gonna be some trouble if they start that shit."

A cop drew his gun and shot into the air.

Until then the older people on the edge of the sidewalk had been looking on indifferently, some stopping to watch, most going calmly about their business, showing disapproval chiefly by refusing to take sides. But suddenly all movement among them stopped and they became engaged.

The youths fled back into the shadows of 124th Street. The cops followed. There was the sound of garbage cans being thrown into the street.

Another shot rang out from the darkness of 124th Street. The older people began to drift in that direction, seemingly without purpose, but now everything about them showed disapproval of the police.

Grave Digger put his hand on the handle of the door. He was sitting on the curb side, away from the ruckus across the street, and Coffin Ed was beneath the wheel.

Four skinny black youths converged on the car from the sidewalk.

"What you mothers doing here?" one challenged.

In the shadow of the doorway across the sidewalk behind them, Grave Digger saw a squat, black middle-aged man wearing a dark suit and a red fez affected by the Black Muslims. He drew his hand back from the door.

"We's just sittin'," he said.

"We run out of gas," Coffin Ed added.

Another youth mumbled, "You mothers ain't funny."

"Is that a question or a conclusion?" Grave Digger said.

Not one of the youths smiled. Their solemnity worried the detectives. It seemed that most of the other youths engaged in cop baiting were enjoying it, but these had a purpose.

"Why ain't you mothers out there fighting whitey?" the youth challenged.

Grave Digger opened his hands. "We're scared," he said.

Before the youth replied he looked over his shoulder. Grave Digger didn't see the slightest motion by the man in the fez but the youths moved off without another word.

"Something tells me there's more behind this little fracas than meets the eye," Grave Digger said.

"Ain't there always?"

Grave Digger got the Harlem precinct station on the radio. "Gimme the Lieutenant."

Anderson came on.

"We're getting some ideas."

"We want facts," Anderson said.

Grave Digger's gaze wandered across the street. The elderly people were collecting in little knots on both corners of the intersection of 124th Street, the white cops were backing slowly from the shadows, empty-handed, but wary. The blazing arc of a Molotov cocktail came down from a tenement roof. The bottle shattered harmlessly in the street. Burning gasoline blazed briefly for a moment and dark figures sprang momentarily into vision, faces shining, eyes gleaming, before sinking back into the gloom like stones into the sea as the blaze flickered and went out.

"There ain't gonna be any facts," Grave Digger informed Anderson.

"Something will break," Anderson said.

Coffin Ed looked across at Grave Digger and shook his head.

"Well, you want we should move around a little and see what we can pick up?" Grave Digger asked.

"No, just lay dead and let the race leaders handle it," Anderson said. "We want the nitty-gritty."

Grave Digger stifled an impulse to say, "What dat?" and caught Ed's eye. Anderson made them hilarious with what he thought was hep-talk, but they had never let him know it.

"We dig you, boss," Grave Digger gave a reply equally as square but Anderson didn't get it.

When he had switched off the radio, Grave Digger said, "Ain't that some shit! Here they got a riot and a thousand cops scattered all over the streets and they don't know how it started."

"We don't neither."

"Hell, we weren't here."

"The Lieutenant wants us to sit here until the answer turns up."

A black stringbean wearing a floppy white hat came cautiously from 125th Street with a huge brown woman in a sleeveless dress. They moved as though they were crossing no-man's-land. When they drew abreast they peeped furtively at the two black men sitting motionless in the parked car, peeped across the street at the line of white cops, and drew in their eyes.

Police cruisers and mounted cops were prodding the traffic on. Voices came from the sound trucks. Jokers were crowded in the doorway of a bar. Inside, the jukebox was braying folk songs.

"It ain't much of a riot, anyway," Coffin Ed observed.

"Too late in the season."

"In this mother-raping country of IBM's I don't see what they need you and me for anyway."

"Hell, man, IBM's don't work here."

Coffin Ed followed Grave Digger's gaze. "He's gone." They were looking for the man in the red fez.

Suddenly a scuffle broke out on their side of the street. The five youths who had challenged the detectives previously reappeared from the direction of 125th Street, propelling a sixth youth before them. One held the youth's arm twisted behind him and the others were trying to take off his pants. He twisted about, trying to break free, and butted his attackers with his buttocks. "Lemme go!" he cried. "Lemme go! I ain't chicken."

A couple of grown men stood in burrhead silhouette beneath the corner lamps, watching avidly.

"Less cut off his balls," one of his torturers said.

"And give 'em to whitey," another added.

"Man, whitey wants dick."

"Less cut that off too."

"Turn him loose," Grave Digger said, like an elder brother.

Two of the youths stepped back and snapped open chivs.

"Who you, mother?"

Grave Digger got from the car and freed the youth's arm.

Three more blades glinted in the night, as the youths spread out.

The sound of the other car door opening broke into the silence, drawing their attention for a moment.

Grave Digger moved in front of the youth under attack, his big loose hands still empty.

"What's the matter with him?" he asked in a reasonable voice.

The gang stood undecided as Coffin Ed strolled on to the scene.

"He's chicken," one said.

"What you want him to do?"

"Stone whitey."

"Hell, boy, those cops got guns."

"They scared to use 'em."

Another youth exclaimed, "These them mothers said they was scared."

"That's right," Coffin Ed said. "But we ain't scared of you."

"You scared of whitey. You ain't nothing but shit."

"When I was your age I'da got slapped in the mouth for telling a grown man that."

"You slap us, we waste you."

"All right, we believe you," Grave Digger said impatiently. "Go home and leave this kid alone."

"You ain't our Pa."

"Damn right, if I was you wouldn't be out here."

"We're the law," Coffin Ed said to forestall any more argument.

Six pairs of round white-rimmed eyes stared at them accusingly.

"Then you on whitey's side."

"We're on your leader's side."

"Them Doctor Toms," a youth said contemptuously. "They're all on whitey's side."

"Go on home," Grave Digger said, pushing them away, ignoring the flashing knife blades. "Go home and grow up. You'll find out there ain't any other side."

The youths retreated sullenly and he kept pushing them down toward 125th Street as though he were suddenly angry. A police cruiser pulled to the curb and the white cops appeared anxious to help, but he ignored them and went back to join Coffin Ed. For a moment they sat untalking, scanning the sullen Harlem night. All the rioters in their vicinity had disappeared, leaving the sanctimonious citizens hobbling along with prim self-righteousness beneath the hot-eyed scrutiny of the frustrated cops.

"All these punks ought to be home doing their homework," Coffin Ed said, bitterly.

"They got a point," Grave Digger defended. "What they gonna learn to cancel what they already know?"

"Roy Wilkins and Whitney Young ain't gonna like that attitude."

"Sure ain't, but it's still putting butter on their bread."

From behind drawn curtains of a storefront synagogue the black face of a grizzly-bearded rabbi peeped furtively at them. They didn't see him because some heavy object landed on top of their car and sudden flame was pouring down all windows.

"Sit still!" Grave Digger shouted.

Coffin Ed was opening his door and dove barehanded to the sidewalk, scraping the heels of his hands on the concrete while rolling over in the same motion. Some flaming gasoline had dripped on the calves of Grave Digger's trousers but when he undid his belt and ripped open his fly to tear them off he saw Coffin Ed coming around the front end on the car with the back of his coat on fire. He stood straight up with leg power only and clutched the collar of Coffin Ed's coat when he came within reach. In one swift movement he ripped the blazing back out of Coffin Ed's coat and flung it back into the street, but his own pants had fallen around his ankles and were burning smokily with the stink of burning wool. He did a grotesque adagio dance getting his feet clear and stood in his purple shorts examining Coffin Ed to see if he was still burning. Coffin Ed had stuck his pistol in his belt and was frantically freeing his arms of coat sleeves.

"Lucky for your hair," Grave Digger said.

"These kinks is fireproof."

They looked like two idiots standing in the glare of the blazing car, one in his coat, shirt and tie, and purple shorts above gartered sox and big feet, and the other in shirtsleeves and empty shoulder holster with his pistol stuck in his belt.

From across the street foot cops and cruisers were converging on them and someone was yelling, "Stand clear! Stand clear!"

With one accord they moved away from the burning car and searched the nearby rooftop with stabbing gazes. The tenement windows had suddenly filled with Harlem citizens watching the spectacle but no one could be seen on the edges of the roof.

17

From the outside, The Five Spot was unpretentious. It had plate-glass windows on both St Marks Place and Third Avenue, flush with the sidewalk like a supermarket. But there was a second wall, recessed from the windows, containing irregular-sized elliptic openings, giving Picasso-like glimpses of the interior, the curve of a horn, white teeth against red lips, taffy-colored hair and a painted eye, a highball glass floating from the end of a sleeve, stubby black fingers tripping over white piano keys.

On the inside these openings were covered by see-through mirrors, in which the guests could see nothing but reflections of themselves.

But it was soundproof. Not a dribble of noise leaked in from the street unless the door was opened. And no one outside could hear the expensive sounds that were being made within. Which was the point. Those sounds were too expensive to waste.

When the two rough-looking black detectives entered with their little friend, no sounds were being made except the hot eccentric modern rhythm by the angry-faced musicians. The guests were as solemn as though attending a funeral. But it wasn't the sight of two black men with an extroverted pansy that brought on the silence. The detectives knew enough about downtown to know that white people dug jazz in utter silence. However, not all the guests were white. There was a heavy seasoning of dark faces, like in the Assembly of the UN. But these black people had caught it from the white people. Silent people surrounded them.

A blond man in a black lounge suit, who was something in the establishment, ushered them to a ringside seat under the gong. The seat was so conspicuous they knew instantly it was reserved for suspect people. They smiled to themselves, wondering how he figured their little friend. Did they look that much like the kind, they wondered.

But no sooner were they seated than the excitement began. The two women who had driven by the lunch counter uptown in a little foreign sports car earlier in the evening, whom their little friend had called "lesbos", were seated at a nearby table. As though their entrance had been a signal, one of the lesbos leaped atop her table and began doing a frantic belly dance, as if spraying the audience with unseen rays from a gun hidden beneath her mini-skirt. The skirt wasn't much bigger than a G-string. It was in gold lamé, looking indecent against her smooth chamois-colored skin. Her long, unmuscular legs were bare down to silver lamé anklets and flat-heeled gilt sandals. Her midriff was bare, her navel winked suggestively, her breasts wriggled in gilt fishnet like baby seals trying to nurse.

She was slimmer than she had looked in the sports car. Seen up from under, she was unblemished, tall, voluptuous, like a sculptured sea dream. Her heart-shaped face pointed to thick audacious lips. Her short curly hair gleamed like blued steel. She wore sky-blue eye-shadow above her long-lashed amber-colored eyes encircled in black mascara. She had gone so far with the sex image she had stumbled on indecent exposure.

"Throw it to the wind!" You knew a colored man said that. A white man wouldn't want to throw all that fine stuff to the wind.

"Go, Cat, go!" And that was a friend. Probably a white friend. Anyway, someone who knew her name.

She had unzipped her mini-skirt and was shaking it down. His face averted, their little friend jumped to his feet. They looked at him, startled. As a consequence they didn't see the other lesbian at the stripteaser's table get up at the same time.

"Excuse me," he said. "I got to see a man about a dog."

"It figures," Coffin Ed said.
"Can't you take it?" Grave Digger taunted.
He made a face.
"Let him go," Coffin Ed growled. "Just envious is all."
Foolishly the blond man in the black suit was trying to push the mini-skirt back into place. The guests whooped with laughter. The stripteasing woman hooked a long brown leg around his neck, encasing his head with the mini-skirt, and pushed her crotch into his face.
The angry-faced musicians didn't bat an eye. They played on, beating out a modern rhythm of "Don't Go Joe", as though a blond man's head caught in a brown woman's crotch happened all the time. In the background, the pianist was walking around the platform in a long-sleeved green silk shirt, orange linen pants, with a red and black plaid Alpine hat atop his head, and every time he passed the piano player he reached over his shoulder and hit out a chord.
The place had become a madhouse. Those who had had dignity lost it. Those who hadn't became hilarious. Everybody was happy. Except the musicians. The management should have been happy too. But instead there was a bald-headed longfaced man rushing to the rescue of the blond man with his face caught in the stripteaser's crotch. It was debatable whether he wanted to be rescued. Whether he was enjoying it or not, the other white people in the audience were emitting gales of laughter.
The baldheaded man clutched a hot brown leg. Immediately she hooked it around his neck. Then she had both their heads beneath her mini-skirt.
"At the trough!" someone yelled.
"Divide her," another said.
"But leave some," a third voice cautioned.
The stripteasing woman became hysterical. She began shaking her hips from side to side as though trying to crack the heads beneath her mini-skirt against one another. With a concerted effort they pulled free, red as boiled lobsters. The mini-skirt fell to the table top. The brown legs stepped out of it, the redfaced men backed away. With one deft motion the sweating brown woman

took off her black lace panties, triumphantly waving them in the air. Tight black curls ran down to her crotch, forming a patch the size of a fielder's glove against the lighter tint of her belly skin.

People roared, shouted, applauded. "Hurrah! Olé! Bravo!"

The door to the street was opened. Suddenly the loud urgent screams of police sirens poured into the room. Grave Digger and Coffin Ed jumped to their feet and looked around for their little friend. All they saw were people on the edge of panic. The happy music played by angry musicians suddenly ceased. The naked stripteaser screamed, "Pat! Pat!" From many throats came a wail like a cry of anxiety — a new sound. Even before they had reached the street, Grave Digger said, "Too late."

They knew. Everyone seemed to know. Pretty boy, John Babson, lay dead in the gutter, curled up like a foetus, cut to death by the lesbian, Pat, who had followed him into the street. He had been cut so many times he bore little resemblance to the exhibitionist pansy of a few minutes before.

The woman was being put into an ambulance backed up to the curb. She had been cut too, about the arms and face. Blood leaked in streams over her black sweater and slacks. She was a big woman, darker than her sidekick, built like a truck driver who could double for a wet-nurse. But she had lost so much blood she was weak. She moved as though in a daze. Two ambulance attendants had clamped the major cuts and were laying her full-length atop the wheel stretcher inside the ambulance.

Police cruisers were parked along the curb on Third Avenue and St Marks Place. People had come from everywhere; from within the houses, from the streets, from private cars stopping in the street. The intersection was jammed, traffic was stopped. Uniformed police screamed and cursed, frantically blew their whistles, trying to clear the way for the Medical Examiner, the DA's assistant, the man from homicide, who had to come and record the scene, gather up the witnesses, and pronounce the body dead before it would be removed.

Grave Digger and Coffin Ed followed the ambulance to Bellevue, but they weren't permitted to interview the woman. Only a detective from the homicide bureau was allowed to speak to her. All she would say was, "I cut him." The doctors took her away.

The detectives went back to the Cooper Square precinct station on Lafayette Street. The body had been taken to the morgue but the witnesses were being questioned. When they offered themselves as witnesses, the precinct captain let them sit in on the questioning. The five young people they had noticed on their arrival, the two black boys and the three white girls who looked like spaceage witches, made the best witnesses. They had been returning up St Marks Place from Second Avenue when he came out of the rear of The Five Spot and set off down the street, switching his ass. They had known he was heading for The Arabian Baths. Where else? He walked like it. Then she came out the rear of The Five Spot too, running after him like an angry black mother bear, shouting, "Police fink . . . stool pigeon . . . sissy spy . . ." and other things they couldn't repeat. What things? About his sex habits, his mother, his anatomy — they could guess. Nothing that shed more light. She had just run up behind him and cut him straight across the ass with all her might. His ass had popped wide open like a sliced frankfurter. Then she had slashed him as far as she could and by the time he had drawn his own knife and turned to fight her off, it was too late.

"She turned him every way but loose," one of the black boys said in awe.

"Cut him two-way side and flat," the other corroborated.

"Why didn't you two boys stop her?" the questioning lieutenant asked.

Grave Digger looked at Coffin Ed but said nothing.

"I was scared," the black boy confessed guiltily.

"You don't have to feel ashamed," his colored friend assured him. "Nobody runs betwixt a man and a woman knife-fighting."

The lieutenant looked at the other black boy.

"It was funny," he said simply. "She was chivving his ass like beating time and he was dancing about like an adagio dancer."

"What you boys do?" the lieutenant asked.

"We go to school," the black boy said.

"NYU," a white girl elaborated.

"All of you?"

"Sure. Why not?"

"We called the police," the other girl volunteered.

The stripteaser was next, back in her mini-skirt. But she sat with her legs so close together they couldn't tell if she had put her panties back on. She looked cold, even though it was hot. She gave her name as Mrs Catherine Little, and her address as the Clayton Apartments on Lenox Avenue. Her husband was in business. What kind of business? The meat-packing industry, like Cudahy and Swift. He made and packed country sausage for sale to retail stores.

She and her friend, Patricia Davis, had come from a birthday party at the Dagger Club on upper Broadway and they'd stopped by The Five Spot to catch the Thelonius Monk and Leon Bibb show. Grave Digger and Coffin Ed knew the joint, in Harlem it was called the "Bulldaggers" Club; but they said nothing, they were there to observe. Nothing had happened there to shed any light on why her friend cut the man; there hadn't been any men present; it had been a closed affair for the "Mainstreamers" — that was the name of their club. She had no idea why her friend had cut him, he must have assaulted her, or maybe he insulted her, she added, instantly realizing how silly the first had sounded. Her friend had a high temper and was quick to take offense. No, she didn't know of any case where she had cut anyone before, but quite often she had seen her pull her knife on men who insulted her. Well, the kind of insults men usually threw at women who looked like her, as if she could help how she looked. It was her own business how she dressed, she didn't have to dress to please men. No, you wouldn't call her mannish, she was just independent. No, she personally didn't know the victim, she didn't remember ever having seen him before. She couldn't imagine what exactly he had said or done to have started the fight, but she felt certain Pat hadn't started it; Pat — Patricia — would flash her knife but she wouldn't cut anybody unless they made her. Yes, she had known her for a long time; they had been friends before she was married. She'd been married nine years. How old she was? That'd be telling, besides, what difference did it make?

The uptown detectives asked only one question. Grave Digger asked her, "Was he *Jesus Baby*?"

She stared at him from wide, startled eyes. "Are you kidding? Is that a name? *Jesus Baby*?"

He let it pass.

The lieutenant said he'd have to hold her as a material witness. But before they had time to lock her up her husband appeared with a lawyer and a writ of habeas corpus. He was a short, fat, elderly black man with a night tan. His skin had grown lighter and become a shade of mottled brown from the absence of sunlight. He had a bald spot in the back of his skull, around which his kinky mixed gray hair was cut short. His dull brown eyes were glazed, like candied fruit, with thick wrinkled lids. He looked out at the world from these old, half-closed, expressionless eyes as though nothing would surprise him any more. His wide, thin-lipped, sloppy mouth connected with a sharp-angled jaw like a hog's and stuck out like an ape's. But some of his flabbiness was concealed by the very expensive-looking double-breasted suit he wore. He spoke in a low, blurred, Negroid voice. He sounded positive and uneducated; and his teeth were bad.

18

When Grave Digger and Coffin Ed arrived at Barbara Tyne's apartment in the Amsterdam Apartments, they found she had been housecleaning. She had a green scarf tied about her head and was wearing a sweaty pink silk robe when she opened the door. She had a dishcloth in her hand.

They were as startled at sight of her as she was at sight of them. Coffin Ed had said they could clean up at his wife's cousin's; he didn't expect to find Barbara looking like a charwoman. And Grave Digger didn't believe his wife had a cousin who lived in the Amsterdam Apartments, much less one who looked like this and smelled so unmistakably of her trade. She smelled of sweat, too, which was plastering her pink silk robe to her voluptuous brown body, and of a perfume that fitted both her trade and her sweat.

Seemingly, her steaming femality had no effect on Coffin Ed. He was just startled to find her scrubbing in the middle of the night. But at sight of her, sexual urge went off in Grave Digger like an explosion.

She had never seen Grave Digger and for the moment she didn't recognize Coffin Ed. The acid-burnt, terrifying face, with its patchwork of grafted skin, was there, but it was out of context. It was beat up, bloody, bruised. It had a body with torn clothing. It was accompanied by another man who looked the same at first glance. Her eyes stretched in terror. Her mouth flew open, showing the screams gathering in her throat. But they didn't get past her lips. Coffin Ed poked an uppercut through the crack in the door and caught her in the solar plexus. Air exploded from her mouth and she went down on her pratt. Her pink silk robe flew open and her legs flew apart as though it were her natural reaction to getting punched. Grave Digger noticed that the pubic hair in the seam of her crotch was the color of old iron rust, either from unrinsed soap or unwashed sweat.

Coffin Ed snatched a half-filled bottle of whiskey from the cocktail table and held it to her lips. She strangled and blew a spray of whiskey into his face. But she didn't see because her eyes had filled with tears and her glasses misted.

Grave Digger entered the room and closed the door. He looked at his partner, shaking his head.

At that moment, Barbara said, "You didn't have to hit me."

"You were going to scream," Coffin Ed said.

"Well, Jesus Christ, what you expect? Y'all ought to see yourselves."

"We just want to clean up a little," Grave Digger said, adding unnecessarily: "Ed said it'd be all right."

"It's all right," she said. "You just ought to warned me. 'Tween you and them pistols you don't look like the Meek twins." She didn't show any inclination to get up from the floor; she seemed to like it there.

"Anyway, no harm done," Coffin Ed said, making the

introductions. "My partner, Digger: my wife's cousin, Barbara."

Grave Digger looked as though he'd been insulted. "Come on, man, let's wash up and split. We ain't on vacation."

"You know where the bathroom is," Barbara said.

Coffin Ed looked as though he'd like to deny it, but he just said, "Yeah, all right. Maybe you can loan us some clean shirts of your husband's too."

Grave Digger gave him a sour look. "Cut out the bullshit, man; if this girl's got a husband, so have I."

Coffin Ed looked like his feelings were hurt. "Why not? We ain't customers."

Ignoring all their private talk, she said from her position on the floor, "You can have all his clothes you want. He's gone."

Coffin Ed looked startled. "For good?"

"It ain't for bad," she said.

Grave Digger had stepped into the kitchen, looking for the bath. He noticed the black and white checked linoleum had been recently scrubbed. Beside the sink was a pail of dirty suds, and standing beside it a long-handled scrub brush wrapped in a towel that had been used for dry. But it didn't strike him as strange in that kind of pad. A whore was subject to do anything, he thought.

"This way," he heard Coffin Ed call and found his way to the bath.

Coffin Ed had hung his pistol on the doorknob and stripped to the waist and was washing noisily in the bowl, splashing dirty water all over the spotlessly clean floor.

"You make more mess than a street sprinkler," Grave Digger complained, stripping down himself.

When they'd finished, Barbara led them to a built-in clothes closet in the bedroom. Each chose a sport shirt in candy-colored stripes and a sport coat in building-block checks. There weren't any other kinds. But they were big enough to allow for the shoulder holsters and still have enough flare from the side vents to look like giant grasshoppers.

"You look like a horse in that blanket," Coffin Ed said.

"No, I don't," Grave Digger contradicted. "No horse would stand still for this."

Barbara came back from the sitting-room. She had a dust cloth in her hand. "They look just fine," she said, studying them critically.

"Now I know why your old man left you," Grave Digger said.

She looked puzzled.

"It's a hot night to be housecleaning," Coffin Ed said.

"That's why I'm cleaning."

It was his turn to look puzzled. "'Cause it's hot?"

"'Cause he gone."

Grave Digger chuckled. They had gravitated into the sitting-room and upon hearing a Negroid voice saying loudly, "Be calm —" they all turned and looked at the color television. A white man was shown standing on the platform of a police sound truck, exhorting his listeners: 'Go home. It's all over. Just a misunderstanding. . . ." At just that moment he was shown in closeup so all one could see were his sharp Caucasian features talking directly to the television audience. But suddenly the perspective changed, showing all of the intersection of 125th Street and Seventh Avenue with a sea of faces of different colors. Except for the prevalence of so many black faces and such bright clothes, and the cops in uniform, it might have been a crowd scene from any Hollywood film about the Bible. But there aren't that many black people in the Bible. And no cops like those cops. It was a riot scene in Harlem. But no one was rioting. The only movement was of people trying to get before the cameras, get on television.

The white man was saying, ". . . no way to protest in justice. We colored people must be the first to uphold law and order."

The cameras briefly showed the spectators booing, then switched quickly to other sound trucks, occupied by colored people who were no doubt race leaders, and various white men whom Grave Digger and Coffin Ed recognized as the chief inspector of police, the Police Commissioner, the District Attorney, a Negro assistant police commissioner, a white congressman, and Captain Brice of the Harlem precinct, their boss. They didn't see Lieutenant Anderson, their assistant boss. But they noticed three people in one truck who looked like types of Negroes in a wax museum. One was a black hare-lip man in a metallic-blue suit, another a narrow-headed young man who might have been demonstrating Negro youth lacking opportunity and the third, a well-dressed, handsome, whitehaired, prosperous-looking man who was certainly the successful type. All of them looked vaguely familiar, but they couldn't place them just at the moment. Their thoughts were on other things.

"Wonder the big boss ain't beating up his chops about that ain't-the-right-way and crime-don't-pay shit," Grave Digger said.

"Ought to be," Coffin Ed said. "He'll never have as full a house again."

"I see they left little boss man to hold down the fort."

"Don't they always?"

"Let's go down and buzz him."

"Naw, we'd better go in."

On their way down the stairs, Grave Digger asked, "Where'd you find that?"

"In trouble. Where else?"

"You been holding out on me."

"Hell, I don't tell you everything."

"Sure don't. What was the rap?"

"Delinquency."

"Hell, Ed, that woman ain't been a delinquent since you were a little boy."

"It was a long time ago. I straightened her out."

Grave Digger turned his head but it was too dark to see. "So I see," he said.

"You want her to scrub floors?" Coffin Ed demanded testily.

"Ain't that what she been doing?"

Coffin Ed snorted. "You never know what a whore'll do after midnight."

"I was thinking about you, Ed."

"Hell, Digger, I ain't Chinese. I just saved her from a juvenile rap, ain't responsible for the rest of her life."

They emerged on to the street looking like working stiffs trying to play pimps, filled with complaints about their broads.

"Now to get back to the station before someone makes us," Grave Digger said, as he walked around the car and climbed beneath the wheel.

"Just don't go by the riot is all," Coffin Ed said, sliding in beside him.

Lieutenant Anderson came into the detective room as they were searching their lockers for a change of clothes. He looked startled.

"Don't say it," Grave Digger said. "We're the last of the end men."

Anderson grinned. "Be seated, gentlemen."

"We ain't beat our bones yet," Grave Digger added.

"We lost our bones," Coffin Ed elaborated.

"All right, Doctor Bones and Doctor Jones, stop in the office when you're ready."

"We're ready now," Grave Digger said and Coffin Ed echoed:

"As we're ever going to be."

Both had finished transferring the paraphernalia of their trade to the pockets of their own spare jackets. They followed Lieutenant Anderson into the Captain's office. Grave Digger perched a ham on the edge of the big flat-top desk, and Coffin Ed propped his back against the wall in the darkest corner as though holding up the building.

Anderson sat well back of the green-shaded desk lamp in the Captain's chair, looking like a member of the green race.

"All right, all right, out with it," he said. "I take it from those smirks on your faces that you know something we don't."

"We do," Grave Digger said.

"It's just that we don't know what is all," Coffin Ed echoed.

The brief dialogue about the prostitute had attuned their minds to one another, so sharply they could read each other's minds as though they were their own.

But Anderson was accustomed to it. "All joking aside —" he began, but Coffin Ed cut him off:

"We ain't joking."

"It ain't funny," Grave Digger added chuckling.

"All right, all right! I take it you know who started the riot."

"Some folks call him by one name, some another," Coffin Ed said.

"Some call him lack of respect for law and order, some lack of opportunity, some the teachings of the Bible, some the sins of their fathers," Grave Digger expounded. "Some call him ignorance, some poverty, some rebellion. Me and Ed look at him with compassion. We're victims."

"Victims of what?" Anderson asked foolishly.

"Victims of your skin," Coffin Ed shouted brutally, his own patchwork of grafted black skin twitching with passion.

Anderson's skin turned blood red.

"That's the mother-raper at the bottom of it," Grave Digger said. "That's what's making these people run rampage on the streets."

"All right, all right, let's skip the personalities —"

"Ain't nothing personal. We don't mean you, personally, boss," Grave Digger said. "It's your color —"

"My color then —"

"You want us to find the instigator," Grave Digger contended.

"All right, all right," Anderson said resigned, throwing up his hands. "Admitted you people haven't had a fair roll —"

"Roll? This ain't craps. This is life!" Coffin Ed exclaimed. "And it ain't a question of fair or unfair."

"It's a question of law, if the law don't feed us, who is?"

Grave Digger added.

"You got to enforce law to get order," Coffin Ed said.

"What's this, an act?" Lieutenant Anderson asked. "You said you were the last of the end men, you don't have to prove it. I believe you."

"It ain't no act," Coffin Ed said, "Not ours anyway. We're giving you the facts."

"And one fact is the first thing colored people do in all these disturbances of the peace is loot," Grave Digger said. "There must be some reason for the looting other than local instigation, because it happens everywhere, and every time."

"And who're you going to charge for inciting them to loot?" Coffin Ed demanded.

19

The Harlem detectives knew him well. They looked at him. He looked back through his old glazed eyes. No one spoke. They kept their record straight.

Jonas "Fats" Little came to Harlem from Columbus, Georgia, thirty years before at the age of twenty-nine. It had been an open city then. White people had come in droves to see the happy, exotic blacks, to hear the happy jazz from New Orleans, to see the happy dances from the cotton fields. Negroes had aimed to please. They worked in the white folks' kitchens, grinning happily all the time; they changed the white folks' luck and accepted the resulting half-white offspring without protest or embarrassment. They made the best of their ratridden slums, their gingham dresses and blue denim overalls, their stewed chitterlings and pork bones, their ignorance and Jesus. From the very first, Fats was at home. He understood that life; it was all he'd ever known. He understood the people; they were his soul brothers and sisters.

His first job was shining shoes in a barbershop in the Times Square subway station. But the folks uptown in the rooming house where he lived on 117th Street loved the down-home sausage he made for Aunty Cindy Loo, his landprop, from pork scraps he got from the pork concessionaires in the West Forties around the NYC freight line, Saturday afternoons when they shut for the weekends. Other landprops and soul folks running home-cooking joints heard about his sausages, which were dark gray in color from pepper and spices, and melted in the mouth like shortening bread when fried. His landprop put up the capital and provided her kitchen and meat grinder, and they went into business making the original "Cindy Loo Country Sausage", which they sold in brown paper sacks to Harlem restaurants and pork stores and professional sponsors of house rent parties. Soon he was famous and sporting a La Salle limousine with a crested hog's head painted on each of the front doors, a yellow diamond set in a heavy gold band. He was known throughout Harlem as the "Sausage King". That was long before the days of angry blacks and civil rights and black power. A black man with a white woman and a big car was powerful enough. But Fats didn't have any white women — he liked boys.

It was only natural that he became a policy banker. When Dutch Schultz was rubbed out, every sport in Harlem who had two white quarters to rub together opened a policy house. The difference in Fats' was he succeeded, mainly because he didn't stop making sausage. Instead he expanded, taking over the premises of a coal and wood shed on upper Park Avenue, under the NYC railroad trestle, for his factory. And when Cindy Loo died, it was all his own. And he lasted longer than most of the other brothers because he came to terms immediately with the Syndicate, and handed over forty per cent of his gross take to the white man who let him live, without argument. Fats had the advantage over other ambitious brothers, because he always knew who he was. But the Syndicate took all of the hard out of the dick, and soon Fats was earning more from his sausage than his numbers. But the Syndicate didn't want to lose a good man like Fats, who didn't make trouble and knew his place, so they made him their connection in Harlem for horse. That was when he had married that tall tan lesbian chick then working in the chorus line at Small's Paradise Inn, who was still his wife. What with his other affairs, keeping his boys apart and out of the way of his lesbian wife, supervising the manufacture and sales of his sausages, the cutting and distributing of heroin for all the Harlem pushers was too risky; and he got out just one jump ahead of the feds by dumping the shipment for that month into the meat grinder with his sausage moments before they broke in the door. Fats knew his heart wouldn't stand too many capers like that so he looked around for something less hectic and had got in on the LSD trade at the start. Now the extent of his carousing was to take a trip with his favorite boy.

He comforted himself like a respectable and dignified citizen.

But he was never caught in a police station without his lawyer. His lawyer, James Callender, was white, brisk and efficient.

Attorney Callender handed the writ of habeas corpus to the Lieutenant and Fats said, "Come on, Katy," and took the tall mini-skirted, naked-looking, hot-skinned, cold sex-pot by the elbow and marched her toward the door. They looked like Beauty and the Beast.

The detectives, Grave Digger and Coffin Ed, testified that they'd brought the deceased downtown, hoping he might be helpful in tracing a deviate called Jesus Baby. But they had found no trace of Jesus Baby, nor could they think of any reason for John Babson to be killed, Grave Digger, who was the spokesman for the two, confessed. They were unaware that the man and his murderer were acquainted; he had denied knowing her and she had given no sign of knowing him except looking. They hadn't noticed her leave The Five Spot for their attention had been diverted by the woman who called herself Mrs Catherine Little doing a striptease. It was obvious she did it to cover her friend's exit, but how could you prove it? Or whether she knew her friend was going to attack the victim, or even guessed it? All they knew for sure was that John Babson was dead; cut to death by the woman, Patricia Bowles, who had confessed the crime. But whether it was self-defense or deliberate homicide was anyone's guess until the woman was pronounced sufficiently out of danger to be questioned by the police.

They were instructed to appear next morning at the magistrate's court to give their testimony, and sent back to their home precinct in Harlem.

Grave Digger and Coffin Ed went back to their home precinct. Lieutenant Anderson was sitting in the Captain's office, scanning the morning tabloids. They carried a flash of the latest killing as well as a trailer on the Henderson homicide. An editorial titled THE DANGEROUS NIGHT charged the Harlem police with dragging their feet in searching for the murderer of the white man.

"I have to read the papers to find out what you're doing," the Lieutenant greeted.

"All we're doing is losing leads," Grave Digger confessed.

"We're as bad off as two Harlem prostitutes barefooted and knocked up. First there's Lucas Covey, who we think rented the room where Henderson was killed, sprung on a writ and now inaccessible. There's John Babson, who had the same name as the man Covey said he rented the room to, dead now himself; cut to death by a knife-toting lesbian who'd been runnnng around with the wife of Fats Little, a notorious Harlem racket man and sex deviate himself. None of whom we're allowed to say as much as good morning to. And the papers crying about 'dragging feet'. It's a drag all right."

"That's why we have detectives," Anderson said. "If all people came forward and confessed their crimes all we'd need is jailers."

"That's right, boss, that's why detectives have lieutenants, to tell them what to do."

"Haven't you got stool pigeons?"

"This is another world."

"Every world's another world. You men have been too long in Harlem is all. Crime is simple here. All of it is violent. If you were on a midtown beat you'd have a dozen worlds of crime."

"Maybe. But that's neither here nor there. Who killed Charlie is our problem. Or Charlotte? And we need to see our witness. What ones that're living."

"I'm beginning to suspect you fellows hate white people," Anderson said surprisingly.

They froze as though listening for a sound so vague it might never be heard again but which warned of such great danger it was imperative they hear it. Anderson had their full attention now.

"It's the fashion," he added sadly.

"Don't bet on it," Grave Digger warned.

Anderson shook his head.

"Then why can't we have Covey?" Grave Digger persisted. "He's got to be shown the body, anyway, whether he likes it or not."

"You had Covey, remember. That's what the trouble is."

"That! Hell, he can still see. He should have been shown the body of Henderson."

"He was shown the pictures of the body of Henderson taken by the homicide photographer, and he said he didn't recognize him."

"Then have homicide send us some pictures of Babson and we'll take them and have him look at them, wherever he is."

"No, it's not your job. Let homicide do it."

"You know we can find Covey if we want—if he's in Harlem."

"I've told you to lay off Covey."

"All right, we'll work on Fats Little instead. The woman who killed Babson was with his wife at The Five Spot."

"Lay off Little and his wife. There's nothing to show she was involved in the knife fight or was even aware of it, from what you told me. And Little stands very high on the political front, higher than anyone knows."

"We know."

"Then you know he's one of the congressman's biggest campaign contributors."

"All right, give us two weeks' vacation and we'll go to Bimini and get in a little fishing."

"In the middle of these killings? I think that's a bad joke."

"Hell, boss, we can't work up any sweat over these killings. We're hogtied at every turn."

"Do the best you can."

"You sound like a statesman, boss."

"Just take your own advice, and don't make waves."

"You can say it, boss, ain't nobody here but us chickens. You mean nobody really wants Henderson's killer brought to trial, it might uncover an interracial homosexual scandal that nobody wishes known."

Pink came into Anderson's face. "Let the chips fall where they may," he said.

Grave Digger's face went scornful and Coffin Ed looked away in embarrassment. Their poor boss. What he had to endure from his race.

"We got you, boss," Grave Digger said.

They called it a day.

The next morning they went to the magistrate's court and heard Patricia Bowles bound over to the Grand Jury and put in five thousand dollars' bond in her absence. They didn't report for duty at the precinct station that evening until nine o'clock and Lieutenant Anderson greeted them.

"While you were sleeping, the case was closed. Your troubles are over."

"How so?"

"Lucas Covey came in with his lawyer about ten this morning and said he'd read in the paper that a man named John Babson had been killed and he wanted to look at the body and see if it was the same John Babson he had rented the basement room to where Henderson had been killed. The Captain had them taken down to the morgue and he identified the body as the same John Babson, known as Jesus Baby, who was known to take white men to his room. So the Captain and homicide and everyone concerned are satisfied that he was the one killed Henderson."

"Satisfied? You mean jubilant!"

"So the case is closed."

"If you're satisfied, who're we to complain? The woman killed him in self-defense, I suppose?"

"Not as we know of. But she has been released in five thousand dollars' bail put up by Fats Little, and moved out of the prison ward at Bellevue into a private room at forty-eight dollars per day."

"Ain't that something?"

"The only fly in the pudding is a man named Dennis Holman who came in here about seven o'clock this evening and said he was John Babson's landlord on Hamilton Terrace and John Babson couldn't possibly have killed anyone night before last because John Babson was at home all night and he could vouch for practically every minute."

"I'll bet."

"Neither the Captain nor homicide nor any of the others concerned like that very much."

Grave Digger chuckled. "Just wished he'd go away and disappear."

"Something like that. But he's all het up. Says John Babson was like a brother. Says he's had a room in his house for three years and that he's supported his wife and child."

"Let's get those *he's* straightened out. Who *he* with the wife and child, and who *he* supporting them?"

"Well, the wife and child were John Babson's —"

"He was a wife, himself."

"Maybe."

"What maybe?"

"And it was Dennis Holman who was supporting them."

"With that kind of investment, it don't seem natural he'd let John hustle white men, not even for the money."

"The Captain and homicide don't agree. You want to talk to him?"

"Why not?"

They went down and took him out of his cell and carried him to the pigeon's nest, a soundproof, windowless room with a floor-bolted seat beneath a battery of lights where suspects were questioned. Dennis had just been down there in the hands of two of the Captain's men and he wasn't happy to be taken back. He was a big spongy man in a sweat-stained white shirt rolled up at the sleeves and black pants hanging low from a paunch; not fat exactly but without muscles, like a slug. He had a round boyish face, smooth black skin with a red underglow, and large popping maroon-colored eyes; he always looked surprised. He wasn't an ugly man, just strange-looking as though he belonged to a race of jelly men. He didn't have a white lawyer to front for him and he had already been pushed around. Grave Digger and Coffin Ed pushed him around some more. They turned up the lights so high he seemed to turn into smoke.

"You don't have to do that," he said. "I want to talk."

He was chauffeur for a very wealthy white man who spent most of his time abroad, so he had little to do. Once a day, generally around five o'clock after John had gone to work, he checked into his employer's Fifth Avenue apartment to see it hadn't been burgled. But most of the time he was at home, he was a home man. Home was a four-room apartment on Hamilton Terrace and 142nd Street. John Babson rented a room and ate with him when he wasn't at work. He did the cooking and cleaning himself, made the bed — beds — emptied the garbage and such. John didn't like housework, he got enough of it at the lunch counter.

"Too cute?"

"No, he wasn't like that, he wasn't mean; he was a sweet boy. He was just lazy out of bed is all."

"But you got along?"

"Oh, we got along fine, we were good for one another; we never had an argument."

"He was married, wasn't he?"

"Yes, he had a wife and child — little girl. But he shouldn't have never married that woman —"

"Any woman."

"Her in particular. She's a slut, just a chickenshit whore. She'll hop in the bed with anybody with a thing."

"Is it his child?"

"I suppose so, she says it is anyway. He could make a child, if that's what you mean. He was a man."

"Was he?"

"In that way anyway."

"How old is she?"

"Who?"

"His child."

"Oh, about three and a half."

"How long had he been living with you?"

"About four years."

"Then he'd already left her when the child was born?"

"Yes, he'd come to live with me."

"Then you took him away from her?"

"I didn't take him from her, he came of his own free will."

"But she knew about you?"

"She knew about us from the first. She didn't mind. She'd have taken him back if he'd gone back to her, or she'd have shared him with me if he'd stood for it."

"She wasn't very particular."

"Women!" he sneered. "They'll do anything."

"Let's get back to the day Henderson was killed."

"Henderson?"

"The white man."

"I read about him."

"To hell with that."

"Well, John left for work at four o'clock, as usual. He worked from four to twelve —"

"He was late then."

"It didn't matter. Four o'clock's a slack time."

"How'd he go?"

"He always walked, it wasn't far."

"And you stayed at home?"

"No, I went downtown and checked my boss's apartment and got something for supper — John wouldn't eat that crap at the lunch counter if he could help it —"

"Tender bowels, eh?" Coffin Ed said gratingly.

Dennis shrugged. "Whatever you like," he said passively. "I always tried to have supper ready when he came home after midnight. I'd fixed some blue-claw crabs a friend had given me — a chauffeur out on Long Island — and a West Indian dish made of boiled corn meal and okra that I'd taught John to like."

The detectives became alert.

"You West Indian?" Grave Digger was quick to ask.

"Yes, I was born in the hills behind Kingston."

"You know many West Indians here?"

"Noooo, I don't have any reason to see any."

"Was John?"

"John! Oh, no, he was from Alabama."

"You know voodoo?"

"I'm from Jamaica? Voodoo is serious."

"I believe you," Grave Digger said.

"Tell us why she killed him," Coffin Ed said.

"I've thought of nothing else," Dennis confessed. "An' God be my secret judge, I just can't figure it out. He was the gentlest of persons. He was a baby. He never had a vicious thought. He liked to make people happy —"

"I'll bet."

"— he wouldn't have attacked anyone, much less a woman or someone dressed like one."

"I thought he hated women."

"He liked women — some women. He just liked me better."
"But they didn't like him, at least this one didn't."
"The only way I can figure it, it must have been a mistake," he said. "Either she mistook him for somebody else or she mistook something he was doing for something else."
"He wasn't doing nothing but walking down the street."
"Christ in heaven, why?" he exclaimed. "I've racked my brains."
"They fought about something."
"He wouldn't have stood up and fought her, he'd have run away if he could have."
"Maybe he couldn't."
"Yes, after I saw his body I understood. She must have run up behind him without him seeing her and cut him so deep it had crippled him."
Suddenly he clutched his face in his hands and his spongy boneless body heaved convulsively. "She's a monster!" he cried, tears streaming from beneath his hands. "An inhuman monster! She's worse than a blind rattlesnake! She's vile, that woman! Why don't you make her talk? Beat her up! Stomp on her!"
For the first time in memory, the detectives were embarrassed by the anguish of a witness in the pigeon's nest. Coffin Ed backed away as though from a distasteful worm. Automatically Grave Digger dimmed the battery of lights. But his neck had begun to swell from impotent rage.
"We can't get to her because Fats Little has got her covered."
"Fats Little?"
"That's right."
"What's his angle?"
"Who knows?"
"Fuck Fats," Coffin Ed said harshly. "Let's get back to you. How'd you learn he'd been killed? Someone phone you?"
"I read about it in the morning *News*," Dennis admitted. "About five o'clock this morning. You see, when John didn't come home I went by the lunch counter and found out he'd been taken by you people — everyone knows you people, of course. I figured you people had taken him to the station here, so I came

here and inquired at the desk but no one had seen you people. So then I went back to the lunch counter but no one had seen you people there either — since you people had left with him. I couldn't imagine what you people wanted with him, but I figured he was safe."

"What did you think we wanted with him?"

"I figured you people was just looking around, looking into things —"

"What things?"

"I couldn't imagine."

"Then what'd you do?"

"I checked the Apollo bar and the record shop and places in the neighborhood."

"Sissy hangouts?"

"Well, if you want to call them that. Anyway, no one had seen you people, so I went home to wait. It wasn't till almost daybreak that it occurred to me that John might be hurt in an automobile accident or something. I was on my way back here —"

"You got a telephone, haven't you?"

"It's out of order."

"Then what?"

"I bought a morning *News* at the Eighth Avenue subway stop and it was in the late news flashes that someone named John Babson had been killed. After that I don't remember exactly what I did. I must have panicked. The next thing I remember was I was banging on the apartment door on St Nicholas Place where John's wife has a room, and his evil landlady calling through the door that she wasn't home. I don't know why I went there. I must of thought of having her go down and identify the body — they were still legally married."

"Were you surprised to find her out at that hour?"

"No, it wasn't nothing unusual about her being out all night; it'd have been unusual for her to have been home. It was hard to trick in the room with the little girl there."

"Why didn't you go down and identify the body yourself?"

"I couldn't bear the thought of seeing him dead. I knew she wouldn't care, 'sides which we were giving her money."

"You knew the body had to be identified."

"I hadn't thought of it that way. I just wanted to be sure."

Then at noon he'd bought another newspaper and standing on the corner of 145th Street and Eighth Avenue — he couldn't remember how he'd got there — he had read where John's body had been identified by some Harlem building superintendent called Lucas Covey. This Covey man had claimed that John was the man called Jesus Baby who he had rented a room to — the room where the white man was killed two nights ago — three nights —

"And you recognized the name?"

"What name?"

"Covey."

"I don't know anyone called Lucas Covey and I've never heard the name before in my life."

"Did you call John 'Jesus Baby'?"

"Never in my life and I've never heard him called that by anyone. I've never even heard the name Jesus Baby. Jesus Baby and Lucas Covey and the rented room and all that, him being killed by someone named Pat Bowles — I'd never heard of her either, and I'd never heard John speak of her, not to me anyway, and I don't believe he even knew her — I knew then it was a case of mistaken identity. Just a plain mistake that got him killed. She mistook him for somebody else. And then Lucas Covey saying he rented him the room where the white man was killed — either another mistake on Covey's part or he was just plain lying. I was standing there on the sidewalk in the blazing sun and I blacked out. Life is so insecure one can get killed any moment through a mistake. And all the time when whatever it was was going on, he was home in bed."

"You'll testify to that under oath?"

"Testify under oath? I'll swear on a stack of Bibles nine feet high. There was no question about it, he couldn't have killed anyone that night — unless it was me. I can account for every minute of his time. His body was touching my body every minute of that night."

"In bed?"

"Yes, all right, in bed, we were in bed together."

"You were lovers?"

"Yes, yes, yes, if you just got to make me say it. We were lovers, *lovers* — I've said it. We were man and wife, we were whatever you want to call us."

"Did his wife know all this?"

"Irene? She knew everything. She could have cleared his name of all those charges, murdering a white man and calling himself Jesus Baby. She came by the house that night and found us in bed. And she sat on the edge of the bed and said she wanted to see us make love."

"Did you?"

"No, we're not — weren't — exhibitionists. I told her if she wanted to watch someone make love, she could fix up a mirror so she could watch herself."

"Did you find her?"

"Find her?"

"Today."

"Oh, no. She hadn't come home last time I was by there; her landlady is taking care of her little girl. So I had to go down and look at John's body by myself. That's when I knew for sure the killing had been a case of mistaken identity — when I saw the way he'd been cut. He'd been hamstrung from the back so he couldn't have run and that was the end. The only one who can prove this is the — the person who cut him —"

"We can't get to her."

"That's what you told me. You can't get to see her and I had a lot of trouble getting into the morgue to see his body when I'm — was — his only friend. That's the way it is when you're poor. The police didn't believe nothing I said — they brought me back here and I been held in solitary ever since. But I can prove every word I said."

"How?"

"Well, anyway along with his wife. If she'll talk. They'll have to believe her — legally she's his wife. And then legally she'll have to claim his body, although I'll pay for the funeral and everything myself."

"What about your own wife — if you've got a wife? How does she feel about your love life?"

"My wife? I put her down before I came to the World. She ain't no help. It's John's wife you need."

"All right, we'll look up John's wife," Grave Digger said, writing down the address of Irene Babson on St Nicholas Place. "And we'll have you confront Lucas Covey too."

"I'll go with you."

"No, we'll leave you here and bring him to you."

"I want to go with you."

"No, you're safer here. We don't want to lose you too, through a mistake."

Interlude

The word "LOVE" was scrawled on the door in dark paint.

The room smelled of cordite.

The body lay face down on the carpeted floor, at right angles with the bed from which it had fallen.

"Too late," Grave Digger said.

"From some gun with love," Coffin Ed echoed.

It was the last thing they had expected. They were shocked.

Lucas Covey had left the world. But not of his own volition.

Someone had pressed the muzzle of a small-caliber revolver against the flesh of his left temple and pulled the trigger. It had to have been a revolver. An automatic pistol would not have fired pressed against the flesh. The body had pitched forward to the floor. The killer had bent over and put a second bullet into the base of his skull, but from a greater distance, merely singeing the hair.

The TV set was playing. A mellifluous voice spoke of tights that never bagged. Coffin Ed stepped over and turned it off. Grave Digger opened the drawer of the night table and saw the .45 Colt automatic.

"Never had a chance to get at it."

"He didn't believe it," Coffin Ed said. "Someone he knew and trusted stuck a pistol against his temple, looked into his eyes and blew out his brains."

Grave Digger nodded. "It figures. He thought they were joking."

"That could be said of half the victims in the world."

Interlude

And then the little orphan boy asked the question in all their minds, "But why? why? why?"

Solemnly he replied: "It was the God in me."

20

Other than the caper with the big white sex freak involving a gang called "The Real Cool Moslems" and some teen-age colored girls — including his own daughter, Sugartit — Coffin Ed had had very few brushes with juvenile delinquency. The few young hoodlums with whom they had butted heads from time to time hadn't been representative of anyone — but young hoodlums of any race. But this new generation of colored youth with its spaceage behavior was the quantity X to them.

What made them riot and taunt the white police on one hand, and compose poetry and dreams complex enough to throw a Harvard intellectual on the other? All of it couldn't be blamed on broken homes, lack of opportunities, inequalities, poverty, discrimination — or genius either. Most were from the slums that didn't breed genius and dreams, but then some were from good middle-class families that didn't suffer so severely from all the inequalities. And the good and the bad and the smart and the squares alike were a part of some kind of racial ferment: all of them members of the opposition. And there wasn't any damn need of talking about find the one man responsible: there wasn't any one man responsible.

He admitted his concern to Grave Digger as they rode to work.

"What's come over these young people, Digger, while we been chasing pappy thugs?"

"Hell, Ed, you got to realize times have changed since we were sprites. These youngsters were born just after we'd got through fighting a war to wipe out racism and make the world safe for the four freedoms. And you and me were born just after our pappies had got through fighting a war to make the world safe for democracy. But the difference is that by the time we'd fought in a jim-crow army to whip the Nazis and had come home to our native racism, we didn't believe any of that shit. We knew better. We had grown up in the Depression and fought under hypocrites against hypocrites and we'd learned by then that whitey is a liar. Maybe our parents were just like our children and believed their lies but we had learned the only difference between the home-grown racist and the foreign racist was who had the nigger. Our side won so our white rulers were able to keep their niggers so they could yap to their heart's content about how they were going to give us equality as soon as we were ready."

"Digger, let them tell it it's harder to grant us equality than it was to free the slaves."

"Maybe they're right, Ed, maybe they ain't lying this time."

"They lying all right, and that's for sure."

"Maybe. But what saves colored folks our age is we ain't never believed it. But this new generation believes it. And that's how we get riots."

Lieutenant Anderson could tell by the first look at them when they came to work that they weren't in a very cooperative state of mind, so he sent them over to the bookstore to check out the Black Muslims.

"Why the Black Muslims?" Grave Digger wanted to know.

"If somebody was to shit on the street you white folks would send for the Black Muslims," Coffin Ed grated.

"Jesus Christ!" Anderson complained. "Once upon a time you guys were cops — and maybe friends: now you're black racists."

"It's this assignment. You hadn't ought to have put us on this assignment. You ought to know more than anyone else we're not subtle cops. We're tough and heavy-handed. If we find out there's some joker agitating these young people to riot, and we find out who it is, and if we find him, we're gonna beat him to death —"

"We can't have that!"

"And you can't have that."

"Just see what you can learn," Anderson ordered.

It was a Black-Art bookstore on Seventh Avenue dedicated to the writing of black people of all times and from all places. It was in the same category of black witchcraft, black jazz and Black Nationalism. It was run by a well-known black couple with some black people helping out and aside from selling books by black people to black people it served as a kind of headquarters for all the black nationalist movements in Harlem.

There were books everywhere. The main store, entered from Seventh Avenue, had books lining both walls, books back to back in chest-high stalls down the center of the floor. The only place there weren't any books was the ceiling.

"If I had read all these books I wouldn't be a cop," Coffin Ed said.

"Just as well, just as well," Grave Digger said enigmatically.

Mr Grace, the short black proprietor, greeted them. "What brings the arm of the law to this peaceful place?"

"Not you, Mr Grace — you're the cleanest man in Harlem as far as the law is concerned," Grave Digger said.

"Must have friends on high," Coffin Ed muttered.

Mr Grace heard him. "That I have," he conceded, whether by way of threat or confirmation they couldn't tell. "That I have."

"We thought you could help us talk to Michael X, the minister of the Harlem Mosque," Grave Digger explained.

"Why don't you go to the Mosque?" Mr Grace asked.

"You know what they think about cops," Grave Digger said. "We're not trying to stir up trouble. We're trying to simmer it down."

"I don't know if I can help you," Mr Grace said. "The last time I saw Michael X was about a week ago, and he said he was dropping out of sight for a time: the CIA were sniffing around. But he might see you. Just what do you want with him?"

"We just want to ask him if he knows anything about someone stirring up these chickenshit riots. The boss thinks there's some one person behind it, and he thinks Michael X might know something about it."

"I doubt if Michael X knows anything about that," Mr Grace said. "You know they blame him for everything bad that happens in Harlem."

"That's what I told the boss," Coffin Ed said.

Mr Grace looked doubtful. "I know you men don't agree with that. At least I don't think so. You've been on the Harlem scene too long to attribute all the anti-white feelings here to the Black Muslims. But I don't know where he is."

They knew very well that Mr Grace kept in contact with Michael X, wherever he was, and that he acted as Michael X's seeing eye. But they knew there wasn't any way to push him. They could go down and burst into the Mosque with force, but they couldn't find Michael X and the only reason they wouldn't lose their jobs was because police officialdom hated the Black Muslims so much. It would be too much like taking advantage of their "in" with whitey. So all they could do was appeal to Mr Grace.

"We'll talk to him right here if he'll come here," Grave Digger said. "And if you don't trust us we'll give you our pistols to hold."

"And you can have all the witnesses you want on hand," Coffin Ed said. "And anybody can say anything they want."

"All we want is just to get a statement from Michael X that we can take back to the boss," Grave Digger elaborated, knowing Michael X's vanity. "Me and Ed don't believe none of this shit, but Michael X can state it better than we can."

Mr Grace knew that Michael X would welcome the opportunity to state the position of the Black Muslims to the police through two black cops he could trust, so he said, "Come into the Sanctum and I'll see if I can locate him."

He led them to a room in back of the bookstore which served as his office. There was a flat-topped desk in the center covered with open books, surrounded by dusty stacks of books and cartons of items, many of which they couldn't identify. Aluminum containers for reels of film were scattered among objects which might have been used by African witch doctors or worn by African warriors: bones, feathers, headgear, clothing of a sort, robes, masks, staffs, spears, shields, a carton of dusty manuscripts in some foreign script, stuffed snakes, sets of stones, bracelets and anklets, and chains and leg-irons used in the slave trade. The walls were literally covered with signed photographs of practically all famous colored people from the arts and the stage and the political arena, both here and abroad, and unsigned photographs and portraits of all the black people connected with the abolitionist movement and various legendary African chiefs who had opposed or profited from black slavery. In that room it was easy to believe in a Black World, and black racism seemed more natural than atypical.

The ceiling was a stained-glass mosaic, but it was too dark outside to distinguish the pattern. Evidently the room extended into a back courtyard, and no doubt it had some secret exit and access, the detectives thought, as they sat patiently on two spindle-legged overstuffed straight-backed chairs, from some period or other, probably some African period, and listened to Mr Grace dial one wrong number after another under the impression that he was fooling someone.

After what he deemed was a suitable lapse of time and a convincing performance, Mr Grace was heard to say: "Michael, I've been trying to locate you everywhere. Coffin Ed and Grave Digger want to talk to you. They're here. . . . The chief seems to think there's some one person inciting these riots in Harlem, and I thought it'd be a good idea for you to make a statement. . . . They say they don't believe you or the Black Muslims are implicated in any way, but they must have something to tell their chief. . . ." He nodded and looked at the detectives: "He says he'll come here, but it'll take him about half an hour."

"We'll wait," Grave Digger said.

Mr Grace relayed the message and hung up. Then he began

showing them various curios from the slave trade, advertisements, pictures of slave ships, of slaves in steerage, of the auction block, an iron bar used as currency in buying slaves, a whip made of rhinoceros hide used by the Africans to drive the slaves to the coast, a branding silver, a cat-o'-nine-tails used on the slaves aboard ship, a pincers to pull teeth — to what purpose they couldn't tell.

"We know we're descended from slaves," Coffin Ed said harshly. "What're you trying to tell us?"

"Now you've got the chance, be free," Mr Grace said enigmatically.

Michael X was a tall, thin brown man with a narrow intelligent face. Sharp eyes that didn't miss a thing glinted from behind rimless spectacles. He looked like he could be Billie Holiday's kid brother. Mr Grace stood up and gave him the seat behind the desk. "Do you want me to stick around, Michael? Mary-Louise can step in too, if you want." Mary-Louise was his wife: she was taking care of the store.

"As you like," Michael X said. He was master of the situation.

Mr Grace pulled up another period chair and sat quietly and let him take charge.

"As I understand it, headquarters thinks there's one person up here who's inciting these people to riot," Michael X spoke to the detectives.

"That's the general idea," Grave Digger said. They didn't expect to get anything: they were just following orders.

"There's Mister Big," Michael X said. "He handles the narcotics and the graft and the prostitution and runs the numbers for the Syndicate—"

"Mister Sam?" Grave Digger asked, leaning forward.

Michael X's eyes glinted behind his polished spectacles. He might have been smiling. It was difficult to tell. "Who do you think you're kidding? You know very well Mister Sam was a flunky."

"Who?" Grave Digger demanded.

"Ask your boss, if you really want to know," Michael X said. "He knows." And he couldn't be budged.

"A lot of people are laying it on the Black Muslims' anti-white campaign," Coffin Ed said.

Michael X grinned. He had even white teeth. "They're white, ain't they? Mister Big. The Syndicate. The newspapers. The employers. The landlords. The police — not you men, of course — but then you don't really count in the overall pattern. The government. All white. We're not anti-white, we just don't believe 'em, that's all. Do you?"

No one replied.

Michael X took off his already glistening spectacles. Without them he looked young and immature and very vulnerable: like a young man who could be easily hurt. He looked at them, barefaced and absurdly defiant: "You see, most of us can't do anything that is expected of the American Negro: we can't dance, we can't sing, we can't play any musical instruments, we can't be pleasant and useful and helpful like other brothers because we don't know how — that's what whitey doesn't want to understand — that there are Negroes who are not adapted to making white people feel good. In fact," he added laughing, "there are some of us who can't even show our teeth — our teeth are too bad and we don't have the money to get them fixed. Besides, our breaths smell bad."

They didn't want to argue with Michael X; they merely pushed him as to the identity of "Mister Big".

But each time he replied smilingly, "Ask your boss, he knows."

"You keep on talking like that you won't live long," Grave Digger said.

Michael X put on his polished spectacles and looked at the detectives with a sharp-eyed sardonicism. "You think someone is going to kill me?"

"People been killed for less," Grave Digger said.

21

It was just the blind man didn't want anyone to know he was blind. He refused to use a cane or a Seeing Eye dog and if anyone tried to help him across a street more than likely they'd be rewarded with insults. Luckily, he remembered certain things from the time when he could see, and these remembrances were guides to his behavior. For the most part he tried to act like anyone else and that caused all the trouble.

He remembered how to shoot dice from the time that he could see well enough to lose his pay every Saturday night. He still went to crap games and still lost his bread. That hadn't changed.

Since he had become blind he had become a very stern-looking, silent man. He had skin the colour and texture of brown wrapping-paper; reddish, unkempt, kinky hair that looked burnt; and staring, milky, unblinking blind eyes with red rims that looked cooked. His eyes had the manacing stare of a heat-blind snake which, along with his stern demeanor, could be very disconcerting.

However, he wasn't impressive physically. If he could have seen, anyone would have taken him on. He was tall and flabby and didn't look strong enough to squash a chinch. He wore a stained seersucker coat with a torn right sleeve over a soiled nylon sport shirt, along with baggy brown pants and scuffed and runover army shoes which had never been cleaned. He always looked hard up but he always managed to get hold of enough money to shoot dice. Old-timers said when he was winning he'd bet harder than lightning bumps a stump. But he was seldom winning.

He was up to the dice game at Fo-Fo's "Sporting Gentlemen's Club" on the third floor of a walkup at the corner of 135th Street and Lenox Avenue. The dice game was in the room that had formerly been the kitchen of the cold-water flat Fo-Fo had converted into a private club for "sporting gentlemen", and the original sink was still there for losers to wash their hands, although the gas stove had been removed to make room for the billiard table where the dice did their dance. It was hot enough in the room to fry brains and the unsmiling soul brothers stood packed about the table, grease running from their heads down into the sweat oozing from their black skin, watching the running of the dice from muddy, bloodshot, but alert eyes. There was nothing to smile about, it was a serious business. They were gambling their bread.

The blind man stood at the head of the table where Abie the Jew used to run his field, winning all the money in the game by betting the dice out, until a Black Muslim brother cut his throat because he wouldn't take a nickel bet. He tossed his last bread into the ring and said defiantly, "I'll take four to one that I come out on 'leven." Maybe Abie the Jew might have given it, but soul brothers are superstitious about their gambling and they figure a blind man might throw anything anytime.

But the back man covered the sawbuck and let the game go on. The stick man tossed the dice into the blind man's big soft trembling right hand, which closed about them like a shell about an egg.

The blind man shook them, saying, "Dice, I beg you," and turned them loose in the big corral. He heard them jump the chain and bounce off the billiard table's lower lip and the stick man cry, "Five-four — *nine*! Nine's the point. Take 'em, Mister Shooter, and see what you can do."

The blind man caught the dice again when they were tossed to him and looked around at the black sweaty faces he knew were there, pausing to stare a moment at each in turn and then said aggressively, "Bet one to four I jump it like I made it."

Abie the Jew might have taken that too, but the blind man knew there wasn't any chance of getting that bet from his soul brothers, he just felt like being contrary. Mother-rapers just waiting to get the jump on him, he thought, but if they fucked with him he'd cost them.

"Turn 'em loose, shooter," the stick man barked. "You done felt 'em long enough, they ain't titties."

Scornfully, the blind man turned them loose. They rolled down the table and came up seven.

"Seven!" the stick man cried. "Four-trey — the country way. Seven! The loser!"

"The dice don't know me," the blind man said, then on second thought asked to see them. "Here, lemme see them dice."

With a "what-can-you-do?" expression, the stick man tossed him the dice. The blind man caught them and felt them. "Got too hot," he pronounced.

"I tole you they weren't titties," the stick man said and cried, "Shooter for the game."

The next shooter threw down and the stick man looked at the blind man. "Sawbuck in the center," he said. "You want him, back man?"

The blind man was the back man but he was a broke man too. "I leave him," he said.

"One gone," the stick man chanted. "Saddest words on land or sea, Mister Shooter, pass by me. Next sport with money to lose."

The blind man stopped at the sink to wash his hands and went out. On his way down the stairs he bumped into a couple of church sisters coming up the stairs and didn't even move to one side. He just went on without apologizing or uttering one word.

"Ain't got no manners at all!" the duck-bottom sister exclaimed indignantly.

"Why is our folks like that?" her lean black sister complained. "Ain't a Christian bone in 'em."

"He's lost his money in that crap game upstairs," sister duck-bottom said. "I knows."

"Somebody oughta tell the police," sister lean-and-black ventured spitefully. "It's a crying shame."

"Ain't it the truth? But they might send 'round some of them white mother-rapers — 'scuse me, Lawd, you's white too."

The blind man heard that and muttered to himself as he groped down the stairs, "Damn right, He white; that's why you black bitches mind him."

He was feeling so good with the thought he got careless and when he stepped out on to the sidewalk he ran head-on into another soul brother hurrying to a funeral.

"Watch where you going, mother-raper!" the brother snarled. "You want all the sidewalk?"

The blind man stopped and turned his face. "You want to make something of it, mother-raper?"

The brother took one look at the blind man's menacing eyes and hurried on. No need of him being no stand-in, he was only a guest, he thought.

When the blind man started walking again, a little burr-headed rebel clad in fewer rags than a bushman's child ran up to him and said breathlessly, "Can I help you, suh?" He had bet his little buddies a Pepsi-Cola top he wasn't scared to speak to the blind man, and they were watching from the back door of the Liberian First Baptist Church, a safe distance away.

The blind man puffed up like a puff adder. "Help me what?"

"Help you across the street, suh?" the little rebel piped bravely, standing his ground.

"You better get lost, you little black bastard, 'fore I whale the daylights out of you!" the blind man shouted. "I can get across the street as good as anybody."

To substantiate his contention the blind man cut across Lenox Avenue against the light, blind eyes staring straight ahead, his tall flabby frame moving nonchalantly like a turned-on zombie. Rubber burnt asphalt as brakes squealed. Metal crashed as cars telescoped. Drivers cursed. Soul people watching him could have bitten off nail-heads with their assholes. But hearing the commotion the blind man just thought the street was full of bad drivers.

He followed the railing about the kiosk down into the subway station and located the ticket booth by the sound of coins clinking. Pushing in that direction, he stepped on the pet corn of a dignified, elegant, gray-haired, light-complexioned soul sister and she let out a bellow. "Oh! Oh! Oh! Mother-raping cocksucking turdeating bastard, are you blind?" Tears of rage and pain flooded from her eyes. The blind man moved on unconcernedly;

he knew she wasn't talking to him, he hadn't done anything.

He shoved his quarter into the ticket window, took his token and nickel change and went through the turnstile out onto the platform following the sound of footsteps. But instead of getting someone to help him at that point he kept on walking straight ahead until he was teetering on the edge of the tracks. A matronly white woman, standing nearby, gasped and clutched him by the arm to pull him back to safety.

But he shook off her hand and flew into a rage. "Take your hands off me, you mother-raping dip!" he shouted. "I'm on to that pickpocket shit!"

Blood flooded the woman's face. She snatched back her hand and instinctively turned to flee. But after taking a few steps outrage overcame her and she stopped and spat, "Nigger! Nigger! Nigger!"

Some mother-raping white whore got herself straightened, he interpreted, listening to the train arrive. He went in with the others and groped about surreptitiously until he found an empty seat and quickly sat next to the aisle, holding his back ramrod straight and assuming a forbidding expression to keep anyone from sitting beside him. Exploring with his feet he ascertained that two people sat on the wall seat between him and the door, but they hadn't made a sound.

The first sound above the general movement of passengers which he was able to distinguish came from a soul brother sitting somewhere in front of him talking to himself in a loud, uninhibited tone of voice: "Mop the floor, Sam. Cut the grass, Sam. Kiss my ass, Sam. Manure the roses, Sam. Do all the dirty work, Sam. *Shit!*"

The voice came from beyond the door and the blind man figured that the loudmouthed soul brother was sitting in the first cross seat facing toward the rear. He could hear the angry resentment in the soul brother's voice but he couldn't see the vindictiveness in his little red eyes or see the white passengers wince.

As though he'd made his eyes red on purpose, the soul brother said jubilantly, "That nigger's dangerous, he's got red eyes.

Hey-hey! Red-eyed nigger!" He searched the white faces to see if any were looking at him. None were.

"What was that you said, Sam?" he asked himself in a sticky falsetto, mimicking someone, probably his white mistress.

"Mam?"

"You said a naughty word, Sam."

"*Nigger*? Y'all says it all the time."

"I don't mean that."

"Weren't none other."

"Don't you sass me, Sam. I heard you."

"*Shit*? All I said was mo' shit mo' roses."

"I *knew* I heard you say a naughty word."

"Yass, mam, if y'all weren't lissenin' y'all wouldn't a' heerd."

"We have to listen to know what you people are thinking."

"Haw-haw-haw! Now ain't that some sure enough shit?" Sam asked himself in his natural voice. "Lissenin', spyin', sniffin' around. Say they caint stand niggers and lean on yo' back to watch you work. Rubbin' up against you. Gettin' in yo' face. Jes so long as you workin' like a nigger. Ain't that somep'n?"

He stared furiously at the two middle-aged white passengers on the wall seat on his side of the door, trying to catch them peeking. But they were looking steadily down into their laps. His red eyes contracted then expanded, theatrically.

This red-eyed soul brother was fat and black and had red lips, too, that looked freshly skinned, against a background of blue gums and a round puffy face dripping with sweat. His bulging-bellied torso was squeezed into a red print sport shirt, open at the collar and wet in the armpits, exposing huge muscular biceps wrapped in glistening black skin. But his legs were so skinny they made him look deformed. They were encased in black pants, as tight as sausage skins, which cut into his crotch, chafing him mercilessly and smothering what looked like a pig in a sack between his legs. To add to his discomfort, the jolting of the coach gave him an excruciating nut-ache.

He looked as uncomfortable as a man can be who can't decide whether to be mad at the mother-raping heat, his mother-raping pants, his cheating old lady or his mother-raping picky white folks.

A huge, lumpy-faced white man across the aisle, who looked as though he might have driven a twenty-ton truck since he was born, turned and looked at the fat brother with a sneer of disgust. Fat Sam caught the look and drew back as if the man had slapped him. Looking quickly about for another brother to appease the white man's rage, he noticed the blind man in the first seat facing him beyond the door. The blind man was sitting there tending to his own business, staring at Fat Sam without seeing him, and frowning as hard as going up a hill at his bad luck. But Fat Sam bitterly resented being stared at, like all soul brothers, and this mother-raper was staring at him in a way that made his blood boil.

"What you staring at, mother-raper?" he shouted belligerently.

The blind man had no way of knowing Fat Sam was talking to him, all he knew was the loudmouthed mother-raper who'd come in talking to his mother-raping self was now trying to pick a fight with some other mother-raper who was just looking at him. But he could understand why the mother-raper was so mad, he'd caught some mother-raping whitey with his old lady. The mother-raper ought to be more careful, he thought unsympathetically, if she were that kind of whore he ought to watch her more; leastways he ought to keep his business to himself. Involuntarily, he made a downward motion, like a cat buzzing to the object Jeff, "Don't rank it, man, don't rank it!"

The gesture hit Fat Sam like a bolt of white lightning and a ray of white heat, and he jumped on it with his two black feet, as they say in that part of the world. Mother-raper wavin' him down like he was a mother-rapin' dog, he thought. Here in front of all these sneakin' white mother-rapers. He was more incensed by the white passengers' furtive smiles than by the blind man's gesture, although he hadn't discovered yet the old man was blind. White mother-rapers kickin' him in the ass from every which-a-side anyhow, he thought furiously, and here his own mother-rapin' soul brother just as much to say, keep yo' ass still, boy, so these white folks can kick it better.

"You doan like how I talk, you ol' mother-raper, you can kiss my black ass!" he shouted at the blind man. "I know you shit-colored Uncle Tom mother-rapers like you! You think I'm a disgrace to the race."

The first the blind man knew the soul brother was talking to him was when he heard some soul sister say protestingly, "That ain't no way to talk to that old man. You oughta be 'shamed of yo'self, he weren't bothering you."

He didn't resent what the soul brother had said as much as the meddling-ass sister calling him an "old man", otherwise he wouldn't have replied.

"I don't give a mother-rape whether you're a disgrace to the race or not!" he shouted, and because he couldn't think of anything else to say, added: "All I want is my bread."

The big white man looked at Fat Sam accusingly, like he'd been caught stealing from a blind man.

Fat Sam caught the look, and it made him madder at the blind man. "Bread!" he shouted. "What mother-raping bread?"

The white passengers looked around guiltily to see what had happened to the old man's bread.

But the blind man's next words relieved them. "What you and those mother-rapers cheated me out of," he accused.

"Me?" Fat Sam exclaimed innocently. "Me cheated you outer yo' bread? I ain't even seen you before, mother-raper!"

"If you ain't seen me, mother-raper, how come you talking to me?"

"Talkin' to you? I ain't talkin' to you, mother-raper. I just ast you who you starin' at, and you go tryna make these white folks think I's cheated you."

"White folks?" the blind man cried. He couldn't have sounded more alarmed if Fat Sam had said the coach was full of snakes. "Where? Where?"

"Here, mother-raper!" Fat Sam crowed triumphantly. "All 'round you. Everywhere!"

The other soul people on the coach looked away before someone thought they knew those brothers, but the white passengers stole furtive peeks.

The big white man thought they were talking about him in a secret language known only to soul people. He reddened with rage.

It was then the sleek, fat, yellow preacher in the black mohair suit and immaculate dog collar, sitting beside the big white man, sensed the rising racial tension. Cautiously he lowered the open pages of the *New York Times*, behind which he had been hiding, and peered over the top at his argumentative brothers.

"Brothers! Brothers!" he admonished. "You can settle your differences without resorting to violence."

"Violence hell!" the big white man exclaimed. "What these niggers need is discipline."

"Beware, mother-raper! Beware!" the blind man warned. Whether he was warning the fat black man or the big white man, no one ever knew. But his voice sounded so dangerous the fat yellow preacher ducked back out of sight behind his newspaper.

But Fat Sam thought it was himself the old man threatened. He jumped to his feet. "You talkin' to me, mother-raper?"

The big white man jumped up an instant later and pushed him back down.

Hearing all the movement, the blind man stood up too; he wasn't going to get caught sitting down.

The big white man saw him and shouted, "And you sit down, too!"

The blind man didn't pay him any attention, not knowing the white man meant him.

The white man charged down the aisle and pushed him down. The blind man looked startled. But all might have ended peacefully if the big white man hadn't slapped him.

The blind man knew it was the white man who had pushed him down, but he thought it was the soul brother who had slapped him, taking advantage of the white man's rage.

It figured. He said protestingly, "What you hit me for, mother-raper?"

"If you don't shut up and behave yourself, I'll hit you again," the white man threatened.

The blind man knew then it was the white man who had slapped him. He stood up again, slowly and dangerously, groping for the back of the seat to brace himself. "If'n you hit me again, white folks, I'll blow you away," he said.

The big white man was taken aback, because he had known all along the old man was blind. "You threatening me, boy?" he said in astonishment.

Fat Sam stood up in front of the door as though whatever happened he was going to be the first one out.

Still playing peacemaker, the fat yellow preacher said from behind his newspaper, "Peace, man, God don't know no color."

"Yeah?" the blind man questioned and pulled out a big .45 caliber revolver from underneath his old seersucker coat and shot at the big white man point-blank.

The blast shattered windows, eardrums, reason and reflexes. The big white man shrunk instantly to the size of a dwarf and his breath swooshed from his collapsed lungs.

Fat Sam's wet black skin dried instantly and turned white.

But the .45 caliber bullet, as sightless as its shooter, had gone the way the pistol had been aimed, through the pages of the *New York Times* and into the heart of the fat yellow preacher. "Uh!" his reverence grunted and turned in his Bible.

The moment of silence was appropriate but unintentional. It was just that all the passengers had died for a moment following the impact of the blast.

Reflexes returned with the stink of burnt cordite which peppered nostrils, watered eyes.

A soul sister leaped to her feet and screamed, "BLIND MAN WITH A PISTOL!" as only a soul sister, with four hundred years of experience, can. Her mouth formed an ellipsoid big enough to swallow the blind man's pistol, exposing the brown tartar stains on her molars and a white-coated tongue flattened between her bottom teeth and humped in the back against the tip of her palate which vibrated like a blood-red tuning-fork.

"BLIND MAN WITH A PISTOL! BLIND MAN WITH A PISTOL!"

It was her screaming which broke everyone's control. Panic went off like Chinese firecrackers.

The big white man leaped ahead from reflex action and collided violently with the blind man, damn near knocking the pistol from his hand. He did a double-take and jumped back, bumping his spine against a tubular iron upright. Thinking he was being attacked from behind by the other soul brother, he leaped ahead again. If die he must, he'd rather it came from the front than behind.

Assaulted the second time by a huge smelly body, the blind man thought he was surrounded by a lynch mob. But he'd take some of the mother-rapers with him, he resolved, and shot twice indiscriminately.

The second blasts were too much. Everyone reacted immediately. Some thought the world was coming to an end; others that the Venusians were coming. A number of the white passengers thought the niggers were taking over; the majority of the soul people thought their time was up.

But Fat Sam was a realist. He ran straight through the glass door. Luckily the train had pulled into the 125th Street station and was grinding to a stop. Because one moment he was inside the coach and the next he was outside on the platform, on his hands and knees, covered with blood, his clothes ripped to ribbons, shards of glass sticking from the sweaty blood covering his wet black skin like the surrealistic top of a Frenchman's wall.

Others trying to follow him got caught in the jagged edges of glass and were slashed unmercifully when the doors were opened. Suddenly the pandemonium had moved to the platform. Bodies crashed in headlong collision, went sprawling on the concrete. Legs kicked futilely in the air. Everyone tried to escape to the street. Screams fanned the panic. The stairs became strewn with the bodies of the fallen. Others fell too as they tried senselessly to run over them.

The soul sister continued to scream, "BLIND MAN WITH A PISTOL!"

The blind man groped about in the dark, panic-stricken, stumbling over the fallen bodies, waving his pistol as though it had eyes. "Where?" he cried piteously. "Where?"

22

The people of Harlem were as mad as only the people of Harlem can be. The New York City government had ordered the demolition of condemned slum buildings in the block on the north side of 125th Street between Lenox and Seventh Avenues, and the residents didn't have any place to go. Residents from other sections of Harlem were mad because these displaced people would be dumped on them, and their neighborhoods would become slums. It was a commerical block too, and the proprietors of small businesses on the ground floors of the condemned buildings were mad because rent in the new buildings would be prohibitive.

The same applied to the residents, but most hadn't thought that far as yet. Now they were absorbed by the urgency of having to find immediate housing, and they bitterly resented being evicted from the homes where some had been born, and their children had been born, and some had married and friends and relatives had died, no matter if these homes were slum flats that had been condemned as unfit for human dwelling. They had been forced to live there, in all the filth and degradation, until their lives had been warped to fit, and now they were being thrown out. It was enough to make a body riot.

One angry sister, who stood watching from the opposite sidewalk, protested loudly, "They calls this *Urban Renewal*, I calls it poor folks removal."

"Why don't she shut up, she cain't do nuthin'?" a young black teeny-bopper said scornfully.

Her black teeny-bopper companion giggled. "She look like a rolled up mattress."

"You shut up, too. You'll look like that yo'self w'en you get her age."

Two young sports who'd just come from the YMCA gym glanced at the display of books in the window of the National African Memorial Bookstore next to the credit jewelers on the corner.

"They gonna tear down the black bookstore, too," one remarked. "They don't want us to have nothing."

"What I care?" the other replied. "I don't read."

Shocked and incredulous, his friend stopped to look at him. "Man, I wouldn't admit it. You ought to learn how to read."

"You don't dig me, man. I didn't say I can't read, I said I don't read. What I want to read all this mother-raping shit whitey is putting down for?"

"Umh!" his friend conceded and continued walking.

However, most of the soul people stood about apathetically, watching the wrecking balls swing against the old crumbling walls. It was a hot day and they sweated copiously as they breathed the poisonous air clogged with gasoline fumes and white plaster dust.

Farther eastward, at the other end of the condemned block, where Lenox Avenue crosses 125th Street, Grave Digger and Coffin Ed stood in the street, shooting the big gray rats that ran from the condemned buildings with their big long-barreled, nickel-plated .38-caliber pistols on .44-caliber frames. Every time the steel demolition ball crashed against a rotten wall, one or more rats ran into the street indignantly, looking more resentful than the evicted people.

Not only rats but startled droves of bedbugs stampeded over the ruins and fat black cockroaches committed suicide by jumping from high windows.

They had an audience of rough-looking jokers from the corner bar who delighted in hearing the big pistols go off.

One rugged stud warned jokingly, "Don't shoot no cats by mistake."

"Cats are too small," Coffin Ed replied. "These rats look more like wolves."

"I mean two-legged cats."

At that moment a big rat came out from underneath a falling

wall, and pawed the sidewalk, snorting.

"Hey! Hey! Rat!" Coffin Ed called like a toreador trying to get the attention of his bull.

The soul brothers watched in silence.

Suddenly the rat looked up through murderous red eyes and Coffin Ed shot it through the center of its forehead. The big brass-jacketed .38 bullet knocked the rat's body out of its fur.

"Olé!" the soul brothers cried.

The four uniformed white cops on the other corner eastward stopped talking and looked around anxiously. They had left their police cars parked on each side of 125th Street, beyond the demolition area, as though to keep any of the dispossessed from crossing the Triborough Bridge into the restricted neighborhoods of Long Island.

"He just shot another rat," one said.

"Too bad it weren't a nigger rat," the second cop said.

"We'll leave that for you," the first cop replied.

"Damn right," the second cop declared. "I ain't scared."

"As big as those rats are those niggers could cook 'em and eat 'em," the third cop remarked cynically.

"And get off relief," the second cop put in.

Three of them laughed.

"Maybe those rats been cooking and eating those niggers is why they're so big," the third cop continued.

"You men are not funny," the fourth cop protested.

"Then why'd you sneak that laugh?" the second cop observed.

"I was retching is all."

"That's all you hypocrites do — retch," the second cop came back.

The third cop caught a movement out of the corner of his eye and jerked his head about. He saw a fat, black man shoot up from the subway, leaking blood, sweat and tears, bringing pandemonium with him. The other bleeding people who erupted behind him looked crazed with terror, as though they had escaped from the bad man.

But it was the sight of the bleeding, running black man which galvanized the white cops into action. A bleeding, running, black man spelled trouble, and they had the whole white race to protect. They went off running in four directions with drawn revolvers and squinting eyes.

Grave Digger and Coffin Ed watched them in amazement.

"What happened?" Coffin Ed asked.

"Just that fat blacky showing all that blood," Grave Digger said.

"Hell, if it was serious he'd have never got this far," Coffin Ed passed it off.

"You don't get it, Ed," Grave Digger explained. "Those white officers have got to protect white womanhood."

Seeing a white uniformed cop skid to a stop and turn to head him off, the fat black man broke in the direction of the Negro detectives. He didn't know them but they had pistols and that was enough.

"He's getting away!" the first cop called from behind.

"I'll cool the nigger!" the front cop said. He was the third cop who thought niggers ate rats.

At that moment the big white man who had started all the fracas came up the stairs, heaving and gasping as though he'd just made it. "That ain't the nigger!" he yelled.

The third cop skidded to a halt, looking suddenly bewildered.

Then the blind man stumbled up the stairs, tapping the railing with his pistol.

The big white man leaped aside in blind terror. "There's the nigger with the pistol," he screamed, pointing at the blind man coming up the subway stairs like "shadow" coming out of East River.

At the sound of his voice the blind man froze. "You still alive, mother-raper?" He sounded shocked.

"Shoot him quick!" the big white man warned the alert white cops.

As though the warning had been for him, the blind man upped with his pistol and shot at the big white man the second time. The big white man leaped straight up in the air as though a firecracker had exploded in his ass-hole.

But the bullet had hit the white cop in the middle of the

forehead, as he was taking aim, and he fell down dead.

The soul brothers who had been watching the antics of the white cops, petrified with awe, picked up their feet and split.

When the three other uniformed white cops converged on the blind man he was still pulling the trigger of the empty double-action pistol. Quickly they cut him down.

The soul brothers who had got as far as doorways and corners, paused for a moment to see the results.

"Great Godamighty!" one of them exclaimed. "The mother-raping white cops has shot down that innocent brother!"

He had a loud, carrying voice, as soul brothers are apt to have, and a number of other soul people who hadn't seen it, heard him. They believed him.

Like wildfire the rumor spread.

"DEAD MAN! DEAD MAN! . . ."

"WHITEY HAS MURDERED A SOUL BROTHER!"

"THE MOTHER-RAPING WHITE COPS, THAT'S WHO!"

"GET THEM MOTHER-RAPERS, MAN!"

"JUST LEAVE ME GET MY MOTHER-RAPING GUN!"

An hour later Lieutenant Anderson had Grave Digger on the radio-phone. "Can't you men stop that riot?" he demanded.

"It's out of hand, boss," Grave Digger said.

"All right, I'll call for reinforcements. What started it?"

"A blind man with a pistol."

"What's that?"

"You heard me, boss."

"That don't make any sense."

"Sure don't."

ABOUT THE AUTHOR

CHESTER HIMES was born in Missouri in 1909. He began writing while serving a prison sentence for a jewel theft and published just short of twenty novels before his death in 1984. Among his best-known thrillers are *Cotton Comes to Harlem, The Crazy Kill, A Rage in Harlem, The Real Cool Killers,* and *The Heat's On,* all available from Vintage.

Printed in the United States
by Baker & Taylor Publisher Services